West of a River

Rambling Reflections
From a Short-grass Country Banker

"So what the heck, if you spend a lifetime in the same territory something interesting is bound to happen."

by Bruce B. Hodson

Cover Picture: by South Dakota artist and mountain man, Dan Deuter, whose numerous works have brought much pleasure to the guests who found the opportunity to visit the Blackpipe Collection, gallery and display, in the enlarged lobby area of the Blackpipe State Bank.

Cartoon pictures by Kenneth Moreland

For further information:
Bruce Hodson
Box 306
Martin, South Dakota 57551

1997 by Bruce B. Hodson

Book set and designed by Bennett County Booster
Printing by Argus Printers

ISBN: 0-9661320-0-9

Dedicated

to

the people of the community
that made it all possible

The Contents

Introduction

At the urging of Horace Greeley, Americans have exposed their exploratory urges and 'Gone West.' Be that for the sheer excitement. In search of a better life. Or to escape whatever conditions that the more congested Eastern colonization had imposed upon them.

So America's rivers became goals to cross. The structure of the United States, with its north-south drainage systems, placed those boundaries at regular intervals like rungs in a ladder. Like moats about the safety of the castle. The other side was always an exciting mystery that needed to be explored. Jurisdictions began and ended at the shores of rivers. And rivers generally ran either south or north. To go west, you crossed a river. And you kept crossing rivers until you found what your heart told you was the place to settle down and make it a home.

Our European settlers first crossed the 'big river.' They were content with the eastern shoreline. And we all know the rest of the story. Each restless generation crossed another river, seeking. Our east river Dakotans refer to the Mississippi or the James Rivers, when they went west of the river. My parents' restless spirit brought them across the Missouri. That river that so definitely divides the Dakotas both geographically, financially and style. Loyalty cements all Dakotans, we love our Dakota and defend it against all comers, whether we are east or west river. But like all close families we also have our friendly family differences. If you are east river, that's special. If you are west river you are special. If you are east river you tend to wear the badges of knee length rubber boots, an adjustable bill cap with a corn seed ad. You love big tractors and Scandanavians predominate. West river flaunts their cowboy boots, wide brim, sweaty and weathered cowboy hat. You let east river raise hogs, you want to raise the cattle. You drive several pickup trucks and wave at every car you meet on the road, usually with the

the waggle of your right forefinger, without taking your hand off the steering wheel.

In this book, I fondly am referring to 'Our West River.' That short grass Dakota country west of the Missouri and east of our beautiful Black Hills. Fully accepting that we have truly great neighbors west of us, whose boundary might be the Cheyenne or Big Horn or Yellowstone Rivers and to them, we are just some more east river folks, who stopped off before arriving at that really great Big Sky country. They like that, we are content with what we have. And this is what I have written about.

Recollections

A selection of memos from the memoirs of a conservative old banker with reservations.

It is not my intention to bore anyone with the dry and uninteresting technicalities of banking, but rather to share with you some of those small events that occurred during my banking years which may be interesting sideline activities. These are stories about the good people I knew and with whom I worked, both from their perspective and mine. I hope to share some of those events of humor and heartaches with you from that period in our lives when rural America was still very spontaneous and unadulterated from the modern day electronic influences.

We must remember not to take ourselves, or this book, too seriously. But then there does come a time in everyone's life when those twilight years provide the luxury of reflective hours. Time to let the mind wander randomly through those previous decades, skipping mindlessly about, early and late, good times and bad, happy and sad. These precious recollections now scramble back and forth through our thoughts without schedule or reason, often prompted by some small event of the day, some spoken word triggering the moment. Momentarily we recapture an instant in our forgotten past, sometimes bringing forth a sudden smile, a blush, a chuckle to oneself or perhaps a tear as we recall a situation we handled poorly. Some thoughts bring forth glorious memories, some jarringly sad and painful.

This book contains a random selection of such events that I have recalled, certainly none of which are any more unique, important or exciting than you have experienced yourself. I do not want to imply that these reflections are anything special, but, hopefully, they may encourage you, the reader, to also recall, reflect and jot down some of those precious, memorable events of your own past. Savor them and smile. I encourage you to share them with your loved ones and, perhaps, with others like myself. If you are the sole repository of such special history, you owe it to those who come after you to pass it along. What the heck, if I can do this, so can you.

The Avocations of Country Banking

When Hod and Em secured the charter for a bank to be established on July 19, 1919, 25 miles south of Belvidere, along the Blackpipe Creek, it was assumed that the new village to be established would be called Blackpipe. Hence the name traditionally chosen for a bank. At the time of the application, there was one trading post and general store already in place on the Blackpipe Creek, approximately one and a half miles north of the present village of Norris, South Dakota.

The Putnam family, who owned that trading post, found it necessary to move off that site on the Blackpipe Creek. They skidded the store building to this new location on deeded land. Their application for the name Blackpipe for the postoffice was arbitrarily changed by the postal department to Norris instead. So by the time Hod was ready to begin construction on the bank building, the site was changed and the name didn't fit. However, since it was still in the lush Blackpipe Creek valley, the bank chartered name of Blackpipe still seemed appropriate. That now made Norris a two-business-place town.

The post office fit fine in the Putnam store except for a short period when Hod provided that service in the bank lobby. The bank also provided the service to the switchboard when a telephone line was later built down from Belvidere through Cedar Butte. This was the established road at that time from the railroad town of Belvidere. Go south, ford the

11

Big White River, thence southeast to Cedar Butte, thence west to the Corn Creek Indian school, thence south six miles to Norris.

To further provide for community needs, Hod built the new bank building twice as big as the bank needed. This provided the extra space for the only community meeting hall which was lighted by brass swing-out brackets with oil lamps for night functions. The bank was likewise lighted by "coal oil" lamps. Living quarters were provided in two rooms in the back.

Later a telephone line was built into Norris from the Rosebud Indian Agency, but there wasn't a connection between the incoming line from the north and this south line. Messages that needed relaying were provided, verbatim, by Hod or Em when requested.

The territory was strewn with hundreds of tons of old critter bones: buffalo, cattle, horses. So in order to provide some cash flow to the community, Hod began buying up hides and bones, which were regularly shipped out by rail from Belvidere.

It soon became evident that if the community was to continue to grow, a convenient source of building materials was needed. Since Hod had previously managed several lumber yards, he built one to the north of the Blackpipe State Bank. He also provided wagon scales for the farmers to weigh their hogs, the coal for sale and such. For weight tickets, the charge was ten cents. Local natives harvested a lot of cedar fence posts and these were also placed in stock in the lumber yard. This was convenient for the ranchers and farmers, who were by now fencing up the open range. Heavy duty, 10 inch corner posts, cedar or pitch pine, retailed at 25 cents. Smaller line posts were 10 cents. Lump coal retailed for $4 to $4.50 per ton, scoop loaded.

The community room was an active place with weddings, dances, home talent plays, box socials, school programs, Christmas parties, funerals, traveling movies and the like. It was a great relief when Hod finally managed to secure a 32 volt light plant with storage batteries and wired the hall and bank. That then allowed the discontinuance of the hundreds of wax candles, with their little clips, from the community Christmas trees and the buckets of sand kept nearby just in case of fire, as well as retirement of the lamps from the walls. It also provided our traveling movie man with a power source much quieter than his usual portable gas-operated generator and/or the hand crank. Until then it was a little hard for us youngsters to hear the adults as they read the script across the bottom of those old silent movies.

Upon moving the bank to Martin, South Dakota, our telephone service was still very limited. I believe there were about seven of us on the party line in 1934. To send or receive long distance calls, we had to make a trip over to the Sasenbery Hardware/Funeral Home to step into the booth and handle the call.

In the height of the dirty '30s, the Red Cross came to Hod in Norris and asked if he would distribute some emergency food and hay for them. This he did for a couple of years, long before the government came forward with anything.

Since there was nothing left for the family milk cows to eat after the grasshoppers took over, and because there was no bottled milk service at the general store, Dad concentrated first on acquiring hay for the milk cows. Children needed milk—period. So armed with vouchers from the Red Cross, he made several trips over into the LaCreek valley of Bennett County and purchased many truckloads of baled hay. These he doled out a few bales at a time.

As for the Red Cross food, there was no refrigeration available, so we used the cellar under the bank as the best place to store butter, eggs, bacon, hams, grapefruit, rice and such; all of it went down there. In warmer weather, it was an after school chore to rub the bacon and hams with vinegar cloth to kill any mold. Potatoes had to be de-sprouted. Hod stored the sacked flour in the lumber yard storage sheds and trapped for mice. The coal that the Red Cross provided went into the lumber yard coal bins since no one could afford to buy any anyway and they were empty. Aside from coal, most folks used ear corn or cow chips for fuel.

There was little similarity between those times and today's culture. Hod found that most needy folks were far too proud back then to accept a hand-out. He could often get a neighbor to take some stuff out for a family in need. On Sundays or after hours, he often drove his old beat-up Studebaker about the countryside to place a gunny sack of food on a doorstep and leave. We all knew full well that the family inside knew he was out there, but he didn't want to add to their embarrassment. It was generally easier to get folks to pick up a few hay bales since no one's pride could stand in the way of a hungry innocent critter who could provide milk for innocent hungry kids.

To sort of round out the avocations, Hod approached the Federal Land Bank people, when the Blackpipe had no more money to loan, and processed loans for qualified borrowers through the FLB agency.

The Community Meeting Room

When Hod and his work crew built the bank building at Norris in 1919, he recognized the real need for some sort of community meeting space. There wasn't even a church in the town at that time, and the school didn't lend itself to such occasions as weddings, funerals, etc. So he committed one half of the new project to a community room. It seemed quite large to a little tyke like myself, but I'm sure it wasn't more than 24 feet wide and about 42 feet long. It had a potbelly stove and a small stage at one end for home-talent plays, school presentations and such. It had an old fashioned player piano and hardwood floors for dancing. All about the walls were kerosene (coal-oil) lamps hung in brass swing-out bracket holders.

Each Christmas there was a community Christmas tree set up all decorated with candles clipped to the tree branches with those little spring clip devices made out of red and green crimped tin. Nearby were several buckets of sand and/or water, just in case. As I look back on it, I'm amazed how few structures were burned up during those years!

We had a large backyard where Dad had built pens and cages for the multitude of captured wildlife presented to him by neighbors. Over the years, I remember a coyote, skunk, weasel, dozens of rabbits, a badger, numerous snakes and seven raccoons. My oldest brother, Herb, was adopted by one old mother coon who loved to be carried around on his shoulder. One evening, while a community dance was in progress, the mother coon got loose. As she scurried across the dance floor looking for Herb, she managed to stir up quite a few shrieks and scrambling. She was really quite happy to find Herb; whereupon, she crawled to his shoulder contentedly surverying the events. Herb's dance date didn't share his enthusiasm and refused to dance a threesome! Herb had to convince the coon it was time to return to her nest.

Some years later brother Herb, with a knack for such things, built our first radio from a kit (that's the way it was done early on). He would set it to play up on that small stage, plug it into one of those tall gooseneck speakers and share the squeaking, squawking, whistles and a few musical presentations from KOA and WNAX. When Herb went off to college again, the community took up a donation and bought one of the first commercial radios. It was a very large thing in a console. They set it up on the stage and gathered about it, especially on cold winter nights. An interesting amazement to all.

Meeting the B.I.A. Payroll

When we first moved into the Blackpipe Valley to provide their only banking service, the government handling of the reservation Indians was very basic. It indicated the influence of the U.S. Army traditions and procedures. The established Issue Stations were similar to small military establishments. The issue was quite often surplus or excess government issue (G.I.). Places in our area so established were Corn Creek Station, He Dog, Cut-Meat (later known as Parmelee), Blackpipe (a.k.a. Norris), Two Sticks, Rosebud, etc.

In these enclaves you would find a domiciled health nurse who dispensed simple care and medicines or referred patients to hospitals at Rosebud or Pine Ridge. There would be the "boss farmer," who would best be described today as a county agricultural agent, to assist and guide the Indians into that field, as Congress was insistent they were to become farmers. There would be a day school with permanent live-in instructors, usually a family man, whose wife might also work to help prepare meals for the students and/or teach. Generally, a large garden was also tended at the school to provide additional fresh vegetables for the school menu. Oh yes, for fresh milk for the students and the teacher's family, a pasture was provided with several milk cows, tended by the family or others. At most sites there were also Indian police who worked under the Pine Ridge or Rosebud departments. Incarceration, if necessary, was usually at those places. Occasionally, the tribes did use the small town jail in Norris overnight.

Once a month was issue day and pay day. Rations, allowances, such as clothing, and pay were geared to coincide. In the beginning the old army pay day methods were used. Those to be paid lined up, were checked off the role and the superintendent or "boss farmer" counted out the cash to them. Later, checks were issued directly. Since many recipients could not write, we would take their thumb print on the back with an ink pad, write their name for them, as shown on the face of the check, and have two witnesses certify as to their authenticity, whereupon we would dispense the money.

One thing was always evident—the Native American Indians had no more trust in that printed check than they had in the white man's treaties, nor did they trust their paper printed money. To accommodate their concern, we had to ship in large amounts of coin, usually silver dollars. It was not unusual for a small bank of our size (approximately $75,000 in size) to ship in $10,000 monthly for this pay day.

Another thing that was evident was that the women usually handled the money. They would pick up the coin and currency and start down the street to do their shopping, laying the paper money out first. Any coin money they trusted, so that went into their separate poke to take home. This shopping could take days. Besides providing for their family needs, it also resulted in a take-home bag of muzza-ska (white iron) coin money they could feel comfortable with. They did classify smaller hard coin as acceptable, but those silver dollars were their favorite.

Well, as I say, we had to make that railroad shipment of $10,000 in silver on a regular monthly basis. We picked it up on an all day drive to Belvidere to meet the railway express. Once in awhile we might get to the Big White River, three miles south of Belvidere, to find that the water was too high to ford the river. We then had to climb up a ladder to a platform attached to a large cottonwood tree, climb into a homemade cable car attached to a steel cable that crossed the stream to another large cottonwood on the north bank. We pulled ourselves across, hand over hand, being mighty careful not to roll a finger or hand between the cable and the pulley. From that point it was a hike into Belvidere to conduct our business and visit friends and relatives.

On one occasion, when Dad and my oldest brother, Herbert, made the money run, they encountered just such a high water problem. They parked the Model T under the south side cottonwood and proceeded into Belvidere. They conducted their business, picking up the coin shipment of $10,000 in silver, and hitched a ride back to the north side cottonwood. Dad and Herb made several trips over the river until they had all ten 60-pound bags of silver delivered to the base of the south tree. It now being late afternoon and time fleeting, they hurriedly loaded the bags into the Model T and headed down the road along the Blackpipe Creek to Norris.

Dad was always one of those people who believed in double checking everything he did and preached this to us often. So it was quite natural for him, a few miles down the road, to tell Herb to crawl into the back seat and recount those bags. Herb announced that there were nine! Dad ordered a recount—nine!! Well, as you might imagine, dad didn't wait 'til the next stop light to make a U-turn and head back. Sure enough there, in the tall grass beside the south cottonwood, sat the tenth sack. I can assume that old sack was saying to itself, "I'll bet a thousand dollars Hod will be right back!"

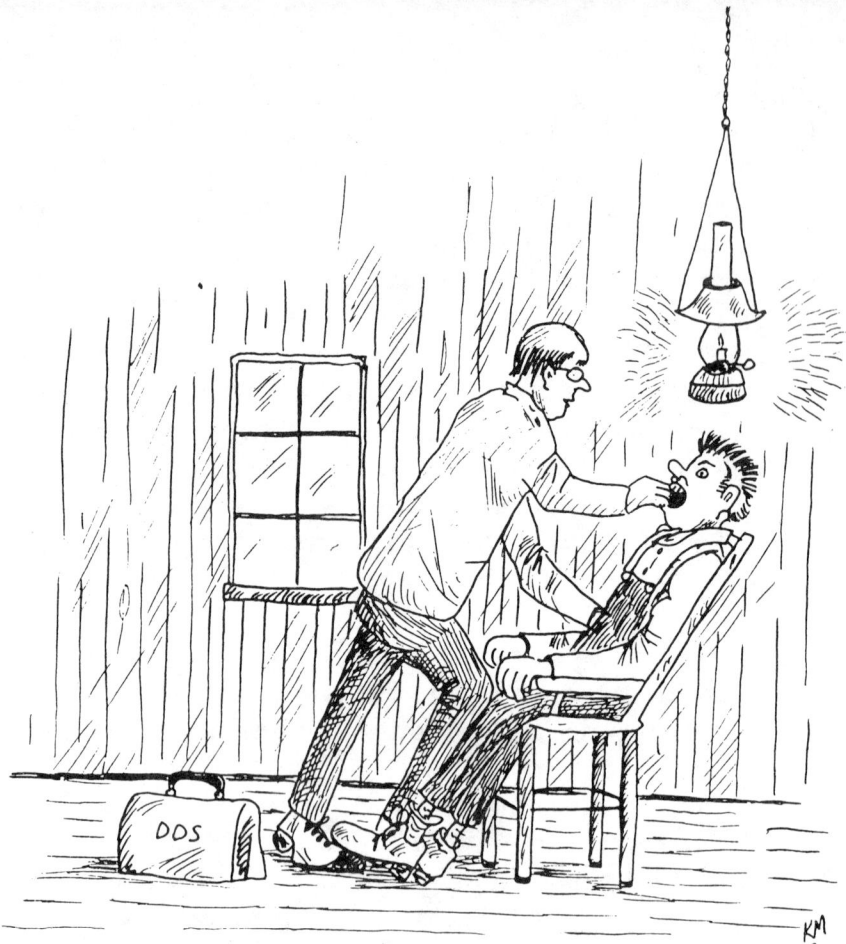

The Traveling Dentist, Circa 1926, Norris

In those earlier homesteading days west of the river, we depended upon all sorts of traveling professionals to provide for our needs and entertainment—the movie man, the Chautauqua Tent shows, the library truck, the pots and pans peddlers, the Watkins man, etc. and, of course, the traveling dentist.

My first introduction to dentistry was, as I am sure was everyone's first visit to a dentist, a memorable occasion. Dental trips for the rest of our lives were governed accordingly.

This old traveling extractor would show up on a very irregular schedule. He would walk about town passing the word of his availability and carry his folding chair and portable, foot-pedal-operated drill into the local boarding house sitting room. He sought out the best available light near the biggest window, near the lamp or, perhaps, an electric light bulb on occasion. The more available light the better. That did dramatically reduce the incidence of extraction errors.

I was playing out in the backyard when Dad called me in to inform me that an appointment with this doctor was awaiting my attention. He directed me to make haste over to the boarding house. Needless to say, I arrived a little tense and nervous; but when Dad told us to do something, you responded accordingly.

In retrospect I am convinced that dentists in those days fit comfortably into that category of sadistic, professional adults who were totally confident that everyone except the male baby knew darned well that circumcision was painless. This same principle was applied to teeth extractions for children. If the patient was young enough, there is no distress when teeth are removed, "Trust me, I'm a professional!"

At any rate, the old dentist sat me down in his hard, non-padded folding chair and pried open my quivering jaws. He hummed out of key as he contemplated just what specific damage he was about to inflict. I am confident that at this point he had assessed the situation and assured himself that here was an opportunity to perform his services for a cash stipend instead of a barter of chickens, ducks, eggs and such, which was often his only revenue. After all, this was a businessman's kid. Go for it!

Whereupon, convinced that he should in good conscience do something fiscally productive or eat his farm products that evening without his 'toddy,' he promptly dabbed two of my teeth with iodine. Reaching in with his unwashed hand attached to a rusty pair of pliers, he proceeded to remove those offending ivories—which, I might say, surprised me. I was laboring until then with the misconception that those teeth were doing a pretty darned good job right where they were. No deadening, no warning, just yank, yank and the job was 'professionally' completed! He dabbed a little more iodine into the vacancies—then realizing that this fiscal opportunity was still ripe—he proceeded to get the flywheel spinning on the foot-pedal drill and done a little prospecting. He plugged those successes with some fillings and sent me back to Dad with a bill for services rendered.

Dad took one look at the $2.85 statement and we both marched back across the street. Dad posed the question that I had already asked myself, "Why take out your frustrations on two perfectly sound teeth?" Dad even suggested, a little caustically, that perhaps the good doctor should move his chair a little closer to the light! The 'doc' stood his ground and convincingly explained to Dad that in years to come that extra space would come in handy for more teeth.

Dad bought that bill of goods, but I learned very young never to trust a thirsty and hungry dentist.

The Jolly Bootleggers

With the arrival of summer, Dad usually set up a tent in the backyard between the bank and our house. Bordering on the north was the lumber yard and then the creek. The whole family, sans air conditioning in our log, sod-roofed home, liked to sleep outdoors. We enjoyed the fresh air, listening to the wildlife activity down on the creek and, hopefully, to the rain on the tent roof. Now, that's the most soothing sound in the world when you live in western dry-land farming country.

Well, as I have stated earlier, when Dad built the bank facilities, he also added a community room, which was used extensively for many local activities. It was the only such place in the valley. There were dances, funerals, weddings, stage plays and traveling movies. At times, we used it for emergency shelter for transients who happened by.

It was during the prohibition days and bootleggers were no different here than anywhere else. It was general practice, when a dance was being held, they would set up shop down along the creek bank somewhere and carry on to supply the consumers' needs. Come to think of it, I can't say they restricted their business hours to only the dances. I think, on occasion, funerals, weddings and other activities were similarly celebrated.

Well, whatever, it was our practice, us boys, to lay out there during those warm summer evenings watching out the front flap of the tent as the cowboys completed their purchases of this happy-juice. They would pass it around among those present, all taking a bit of a nip, then look carefully about to find a safe hiding place for their jug. This usually was quite handy in, under or around some of the lumber piles, shingles or piles of posts. Of course, you have already guessed the next activity. That's when our own free enterprise took over. One of us would dash out just as soon as the coast was clear and retrieve the cache. We would slip it under the edge of the tent and lay back waiting for another recovery.

Come very early morning when most other folks were still sleeping, we would pour all the leftover liquids together into full pints, push the cork back in and meet the bootleggers down by the creek. We got a nickel for the empties and a quarter for the filled ones.

We always consoled ourselves that we were in our own way helping some folks stay sober! Sometimes, when those cowboys returned to find their jug missing, it did lead to some fights with their buddies over who was responsible for misplacing the bottle—that was interesting, too!

The Traveling Movie Man

We had the usual traveling tent shows that came by each year, like the M&M Players, a good, clean, family show, which everyone really enjoyed. The boxes of taffy, sold during intermission, sometimes had lucky slips inside that were good for prizes they handed out at the stage front.

One of the first dramatic entertainments which we always looked forward to was the traveling movie man! If it was a nice warm summer evening, he would set up on the sod north of the bank building, and show the movie upon the white painted metal siding of the building. The siding was imitation cement block design, so the picture showed a somewhat pebbly character, but no one objected. Admission was very cheap and everyone sat around on the ground. If the season called for it, the show was projected on a screen inside the hall. Dad had built saw horses with planks across them for seating. It was always a packed house. Anyone who showed up and could not afford the ticket was let inside anyway. At the end of every reel, the lights had to come on again, while he changed and rewound the reel. The movie man carried with him a portable gasoline powered generator. It made a lot of noise, but with silent movies, who cared? Anyway, every few feet was another adult reading out loud the words at the bottom of the screen for the children and/or adults about them who couldn't read. Sometimes I was a little disappointed with the actual script, preferring to make up some rather exciting words of my own that I really thought fit the activity better than what they read to me.

Of course, the extra entertainment of the piano player, usually the movie man's wife, would accompany the screen activity with a constant rendition of proper music to fit the chase scene, the "icky" love scenes, etc. Every boy watching supplied the "bang, bang" for the guns. It was easy for everyone there to get caught up in the spirit of the moment! Community involvement?

When the first real honest-to-goodness theaters were built in the territory, those great old traveling movie shows became a thing of the past. They sure brought a lot of excitement and pleasure to us small town country folks while they lasted.

The traveling Chautauqua shows continued to make the circuit for a few more years, but the World War II events seemed to close them out. Many old timers out here still think of them nostalgically.

The Powwow Speaker

My brother Herb likes to tell the story about the time when one of the Statehouse politicians came to the Blackpipe valley to solicit the Indian votes and they had a powwow and feed at their round-house meeting hall.

The local Chief rose first to give a flowery introduction and had the crowd all warmed up and excited before the guest arose to make his address. The politician started out with a rousing rendition of their civil rights, their treaty rights and how happy they must be now that they were finally allowed to vote, etc.

Every once in awhile one of the natives would rise up in the crowd and shout "Shunka Cheselee!" The crowd would cheer and clap. It really fired up the politician. The more he promised, the more often he would hear "Shunka Cheselee!" accompanied by more cheering and clapping. It inspired him to his greatest heights, he groped for his most eloquent words. He continued to be rewarded with a rousing "Shunka Cheselee!" and more applause.

In summation he went back over his best points, once more promised his undying efforts on their behalf and sat down to a thunder of shouts of "Shunka Cheselee!"

After the speech a typical tribal feast of native dishes was served along with a smoke on the pipe. When the politician stood to leave, he was escorted to the door by his host who cautioned him to be careful walking back to his car—especially careful not to step in the "Shunka Cheselee."

Sometimes Small Comforts Mean A Lot

I remember back to those happier days of childhood in the Blackpipe Valley and how some insignificant little things will stay with you.

In those days, everyone had an outhouse at the end of the path. In that one or two-holer was the usual 'Sears-Sawbuck' catalog from last season. The slick pages were the last to go. Occasionally a box of corn cobs broke the routine. I am sure that some liberal citizens thought that those used cobs were 'for the pits,' but the more conservative folks would have a cardboard box in the corner into which these expended items were saved. A few days drying out and they still made excellent fuel for the cookstove. And then of course there was always the usual 'poking stick.' For those inquiring minds who must know, yes, that's how the cliche "getting the dirty end of the stick," evolved.

Given adequate time to make the trip, we kids all liked to run over to the outhouse behind the general store. You see, they saved all those paper wrappers off of the oranges and similar fruit, put them in a cardboard box and used them to supplement the catalog. Now that was the ultimate in comfort and class. It just didn't come any better than that!

While on the subject, it seems fitting that I mention that all history of the famous outhouse was not calm, serene and relaxing. I recall the summer when the rattlesnakes moved into the pit below our facility. It wouldn't have been so bad, but it was getting close to that time when the structure needed to be moved to a new, deeper receiving area. So it was a bit of a concern whether the lower residents at that moment were of greater length than the drop zone. All sorts of horror stories were conjured up to the younger siblings as to just how far one of them critters could jump. Each time we told the story the critters got longer as the distance got shorter and the accumulation grew. In other words, it was one chore that we learned to expedite!

In very simple terms, there was very little standing in line to use the facility. No one complained of constipation. The constant buzzing noise during this exercise surely kept your mind on what the trip was all about. We tried all sorts of old-time remedies to encourage them to leave, yet the visitors stayed for about six weeks. Then, just as mysteriously as they arrived, they were gone. Now that's what you call real relief. I guess even snakes will only take about so much of that stuff—politicians take note.

Politicians and alligators have a lot in common. If you swat them with a stick they don't go away, they eat your stick. To get close enough to examine their differences, you need to stuff your stick into their mouths, vertically!

The Roman Coin, Circa 1932, Norris, S.D.

Mr. Frank Pinkham was in today to show Dad an interesting find he had. Mr. Pinkham lived about 12 miles southeast of Norris, in Bennett County, near the headwaters of the Blackpipe Creek. On his place he has a small outbreak of sandhills.

Frank had been out checking on things a few days before. When he got off his horse to check something, he spotted an unusual coin lying there in the sand. He picked it up. Since the Blackpipe State Bank lobby had always been a community display spot of interesting things, he thought that Hod would like to see it.

We all had occasion to look at and hold the coin. To best describe it, it was a fairly thick type coin, about the size of a nickel, perhaps a little smaller. It appeared to be bronze or a similar color metal. On one side it had a horse's head and on the other side a man's head. We could not make out a date, but there was some sort of lettering. It was not neatly rounded as we know coins to be today. Perhaps you would call it generally a round coin, however. The heads of both the horse and man were thicker than the rest of the coin.

We had quite a collection of currency and coin that had been given to Dad for a lobby display. It had been gathered up throughout the world by the returning World War I boys, but we had never seen one like this. Our coin books were too limited to be of help to Frank.

Well, whatever, this has always left me mystified. Just what would have caused a definitely Roman type coin to become lost so far from home? I have since seen several displays of Caesar coins, and they sure fit my memory of that coin of Frank's. Some few years later Frank passed away. I never again heard what became of that bit of local history. He did have relatives in the area; perhaps they found the answer later. It's also an interesting coincidence that on the adjoining ranch of William Dale, they later found a very large, high quality meteor. It is now on display at the Rapid City museum of the South Dakota School of Mines and Technology.

Hod's Christmas Turkeys

As Related to me by One of Our Oldest Customers

One of our oldest customers was in today visiting about old times and about his early-day banking activities with Dad. He wondered if I recalled Dad telling me about "Hod's Christmas Turkey Trip."

Actually, I vaguely remembered something Dad had told me, but I pressed my visitor for more details.

It seems that in the very earliest days of Dad's banking at Belvidere with his brother-in-law, Leonard Pier, they decided it would be nice to build a little good will and PR with some of the newest settlers to the area. They wanted to welcome the settlers by presenting them with a Christmas turkey. Nothing less would do but to acquire some dressed turkeys for the purpose. Then it occurred to Hod and L.A. that perhaps the turkeys wouldn't keep too well without refrigeration until these folks might come to town, or that they might not come to town at all before the big day.

Hod saddled up his big, black, green-broke saddlehorse, tied all the turkeys he could to the saddle and headed out. The bumping turkeys and the unusual nature of the trip

31

didn't add any patience to that green studhorse, and he became unusually restive. For the first four or five homesteads Hod visited, the stud never broke stride, running full-blast, non-stop, snorting and pitching. Hod just started yelling at the top of his lungs as soon as the homestead came in sight to call them out. Then, as he struggled to put the stud into a big circle past the claim shack, he would toss off a turkey, wave and continue on to the next homestead. There was usually a shack on every quarter section. He was down to the last couple of turkeys before the black stud entered into the spirit of the occasion and Dad could stop long enough for a cup of coffee and his "Welcome to Dakota" speech.

Old Home Remedies

It was around the time that I was five years old that I first became aware of the great powers of turpentine. The fellows who hung out at the filling station down the street gathered us uninitiated young citizens to the rear of the repair shop. There we discovered they had captured a stray alley tomcat. Their explanation for his capture was that this citizen had been making a nuisance of himself about the village during those hours when the rest of us respectable citizens were trying to sleep. It was their intention to demonstrate to this cat that such behavior was unacceptable and that he should consider changing this bad habit. The events that followed convinced me that were I that cat, I would indeed restructure those activities; but then, I was only a pre-puberty, five-year-old at the time.

So, here we find Joe holding this cat, whereupon Ed proceeded to apply some vigorous and thorough scrubbing to that bald spot below his tail, with a corn cob. Then Ted steps forward and, with a flourish and "ta-da", splashes a relatively modest amount of turpentine to the prepared area—man-oh-man!

I never saw such a bundle of energy before in my life! One loud squall from that cat and all hell broke loose. With his front wheels tearing up a cloud of dust, his rear legs sticking straight up into the air and his rear brake skidding along behind—such a sudden explosion of activity you never saw!

With hair standing on end, steely eyes bulging, determined jaw set—that citizen headed west. Ms. Taylor was just coming out the outhouse door as the tornado went by. She screamed louder than that cat and slammed the door again. Through the junk car lot, in one door of that old Willys-Knight body and out the other—through the backyard, scattering chickens right and left—under mom's clothesline, right past the nose of Joe's sleepy coon hound—heading for the school yard, straight between the merry-go-round and that giant swing—across the 'one-o-cat' diamond, past the school horse barn—in two minutes flat, that cat disappeared over the creek bank nearly a quarter of a mile from where the demonstration started. Yowls reverberated from the creek banks for several more minutes interspersed with violent splashing of creek water.

That demonstration was profound, believe me! We just stood there with our mouths open for several minutes. Finally Oswald said, "Man, did you see that cat!?" The rest of us just nodded. Yes, we were properly impressed! Ted was happy that their demonstration had gone off without a hitch.

The rest of my life I studied on the mechanics of that demonstration. How anything could make such steady forward progress with only front wheel drive working, and with the rear brake on!—just imagine what could happen if he had released those brakes and turned on the rear drive! Yes, needless to say, young as I may have been, I was properly impressed. You know, I have noticed this through life, there really isn't any lesson quite so impressive as a real life, hands-on demonstration. This is especially true when all the components are in perfect working order and when the educators know just the right application of the catalyst in a truly professional fashion!

I am convinced that turpentine truly is a wonder fuel. Now I began to realize why my Dad also had an affinity for turpentine. Every time Dad wounded himself while carpentering or whatever, he would grab the turpentine, douse it on the open wound, wrap his handkerchief around it and go back to work. Often I watched in fascination as he went on with the chore just as if nothing had happened. I secretly wondered, and perhaps even hoped just a little bit, that I might be around when he wounded himself in the posterior region. Not wishing him any bad luck, you understand, but I knew that accidents do happen. As with all five-year-olds, I had great respect for my Dad. He could do anything. I was willing to bet anyone, should that occasion ever arise, that given the same opportunity and fuel, my Dad could out-distance that old cat any day!

I recall vividly one time when our old dog, Toots, came home with a tear in her ear (probably from having been someplace she shouldn't). Well, Dad casually grabbed his cure-all remedy and sloshed some on that ear. Man-oh man! That cat had better not ever tangle with our old dog! Toots cleared that dog-proof pen without touching a hair. We didn't see her again for three days! We did get occasional reports from folks who swore they'd seen a strange dog in the creek doing the Australian crawl—no dog-paddling for our dog! One fellow said he just couldn't believe how long a dog could hold its breath underwater! One report was that they thought she was diving for carp.

As I study back over those lessons, I can't help but wonder if it's too late to propose a study on turpentine as a substitute wonder fuel.

At another time in a different chapter I will discuss one other lesson I learned at the filling station campus. This was the time they demonstrated the amazing inertia that can be generated by a sleepy old dog by just applying a few empty tin cans to the tail with binder twine!

You know, I spent many, many hours down along that creek through the village, but I could never figure out why all those animals seemed to be in such a mad rush to get there.

I suppose I could have volunteered for that cob-turpentine treatment and discovered it out for myself, but what the heck, I was only five years old, after all; and I hadn't figured out the Santa Claus mystery yet either. I decided that some of these mysteries could be addressed again—when I was six.

I understood that Dad's car ran on liquid fuel, so I accepted fairly well how turpentine could produce some combustible energy. Those empty tin cans, now, that was a mystery. I did consider for awhile stockpiling tin cans to get in on the ground floor of a great future.

You know, come to think of it, that same filling station staff also tied tin cans to the back of Joe's and Mary's old lizzie when they got married. Do you suppose that was another demonstration? But of what? Speed? Inertia? Endurance, or what? Needless to say, I was relieved that they did not head for the creek bank!

Despite getting us into trouble sometimes, we don't really give enough credit to all the pleasures that our nose brings to our lives. Remember Mom's fresh bread? how about new mown hay? choke-cherry blossoms? or your gals perfume on your first date? how about apple pie? and surely in there we must place that exhilerat-ing special smell of the Dakota prairie after a thunder storm at the end of a hot dry day!

Pheasants:
Sometimes You Win, Sometimes You Lose

If I were to try and relate all the pheasant stories of the community, it would take a separate book to do the subject justice. Just as an example, here are two very true stories involving local prominent citizens.

The first event came about when one of our county government officials was stopped by the local warden early one summer day while driving about the beautiful countryside. Knowing each other for many years, it was only natural that on such a pleasant day a roadside visit was in order. However, before they covered the usual subject of the weather, the good crops and who was running for county commissioner this term, that only-stunned pheasant under the government official's pickup seat recuperated and began to thrash about. Under rare circumstances like that, just what can you say that fully covers the situation? An invitation to supper didn't cut it. They did have to get a different justice of the peace to handle the case however.

All such activities don't always wind up in such a legally complicated fashion. I am reminded of an incident during the tough times over at Norris, when one unfortunate farmer was just trying to feed his family with a few early season pheasants, only to be interrupted by the new game warden in the county. There was no need to dispute the facts or wish his kids weren't still hungry. That's the way things turn out sometimes. The warden confiscated the shotgun and the birds, wrote a ticket to appear and left for town.

In Norris the warden took the precaution to lock his patrol car, with evidence inside, in the only garage in town for the evening. He went across the street for supper and rented a room for the night.

Upon rising next morning and after his usual bacon and eggs, the warden retrieved his auto to head back to the county seat, only to learn that some mysterious, very hungry scoundrel had broken into the garage and car trunk and divested him of the evidence. One of those rare coincidences, I am sure, but the farmer was happy to get his shotgun back, when the case was dismissed for lack of evidence.

The Mortgaged Homestead

During the dust bowl '30s, among the families who had to toss in the towel and move away was a homesteader who lived near Cedar Butte. It was sure no disgrace since there just wasn't any way that anyone could survive with a family under those conditions.

At any rate, this homesteader came in to see Dad and explained that he had to try somewhere else. All he had that he could pay on his account was the title to the quarter of land he owned at the edge of the badlands. He wanted to deed that to the bank to apply to his account.

He and Dad went about the process and considered the matter done, that is until our examiners came around. Even though the bank only had $400 against the 160 acres, the examiners refused to let us throw good money after the bad by paying taxes on that land.

Dad sure hated to have the bank's name listed in the local newspaper for unpaid taxes, so he made up a deed for the land and sent it to the Mellette County Treasurer. Shortly thereafter we got back a letter from the County Commissioners stating that they had all the tax land they wanted and refused the deed.

A few years later, when the weather started to turn around, a land agent for the Berry Ranch came around and offered to buy the land for almost enough to cover the debt, interest and accrued taxes. Dad sold it quick.

Phillip's Pet

Phillip was always a practical joker. One day while walking home, he managed to catch a real nice sized rattler.

Then he tied the shoestring to a willow stick about four feet long. He tied a shoestring loop around its neck just back of the head and was teaching it to lead, or at least to take the lead or something. Whatever. After a short spell it became evident that the snake just wasn't cooperating and, sure as the devil, he wasn't going to make it home in time to milk at that pace. For that matter, he just couldn't see any of his family being extremely happy with his pet anyway.

Opportunity quickly presented itself. As he crossed the creek near the settlement, he became aware that one of his friends was singing loudly from his sweat lodge. He was cooking out his hangover.

Phillip had no problem sneaking up on the lodge, raising a flap and kicking his pet inside. Phillip said he had a full hundred yards head start by the time the hides exploded and his now quite sober friend decided he had sweat enough.

Phillip was glad that he wasn't leading his pet any longer. There is no way that darned snake could have kept up with his progress for the next two miles. After all, he had given it a good home.

The Initiation of Manhood

This mid-day started out just like every other dull, warm, summer day in a small town such as Norris. Our old dog was seeking a cool shady spot to take a snooze. The birds were doing their tour of the weed patch beside the garden grabbing a few bugs. The flies were lazily buzzing about. Our milk cow was chewing her cud under the big old elm tree back of the house. If anything was out of the ordinary, I sure failed to pick up on it, but as history will record, there were big events in the making, unknown to a young nine year old like me—things that were to shape my life for many years to come. Recorded here is the best recollection I have as to just how those events evolved.

First off, Mom called brother Kenny and me in from our chores to tell us that we were invited to go over to Bob's mother's house for a stag party. A stag party? What the hell is a stag party? To even my 11 year old brother, this was a new one. A stag party, you say. Oh well, a party is a party. "But what about these chores Dad has laid out for us?" my brother asked. "Yeah, what about them, Mom?" I chimed in. Dad stuck his head out the door to inform us it was no big deal, we could finish those chores tomorrow. That, right there, should have made us suspicious. Dad never took doing chores lightly, but, then, he really didn't dismiss them either. After all, sure as heck, they'd still be there tomorrow.

Well, anyway, we didn't have any trouble dropping those

hoes and running into the house to wash up and change clothes. Again I might have been alerted this wasn't the usual party because Mom didn't insist I put on my usual party outfit. You know the one, they used to call it the Little Lord Fauntleroy get-up. Lordy, how that used to get us razzed. You remember, it was a light tan silk blouse with ruffles and large fancy buttons down the front and more ruffles about the neck and cuffs with a big flouncy silk bow around the neck to make sure you didn't open that collar button for some fresh air. For trousers you wore those brown corduroy, knee-length pants, and the shoes were strap sandals with knee-length stockings. Remember that outfit? Well, enough of this fashion show. To make my point, it was evident early on this party wasn't going to be one of those high society affairs. That in itself relaxed us considerable. So, what the heck, let's head for the party.

As Kenny and I made our way towards the path to Bob's house, across the creek, we met up with the rest of our gang, Vince, Fizzle, Carl, Will and Bert. It was beginning to look like this might be a pretty well organized party after all. Hastily conceived, perhaps, but nonetheless organized.

As we strolled down the path, we were all speculating what the happy occasion could be that prompted this party. Bob's birthday was last month, and, for that matter, how come there were no girls invited? Carl offered, in his older, wiser fashion, that he thought not inviting girls was what distinguished a party as a stag party. In that case, it sounded great to us. Not having to dance to that victrola music with your own sister or anyone else's sister would be a great party, so we thought.

Along the way we checked on those bird nests we were all watching for new hatchlings, stopped at the old bridge-plank creek crossing to observe the pollywogs and baby horseshoe crabs and skipped a few rocks across the water.

Bob's mom was the Bureau of Indian Affairs health nurse for the local citizenry. They lived in one of those old standard government-built buildings, designed with a small receiving room and office and living quarters. It was similar to the nearby "Boss Farmer's" quarters and the day school, all of which rounded out the BIA headquarters for the Blackpipe District. All the buildings were standardized to the identical prints used everywhere by the BIA, including a cistern for the run-off water from the sheet metal shingle roofs. As there was a plentiful supply of good, cold well water available from shallow hand-dug wells at Blackpipe, the cistern was not used; but standardization was a must, and like it or not, every government BIA structure was equipped with that cistern.

When we arrived at Bob's place, he was outside the house, lying on his belly doing his favorite self-entertainment activity. He was peering down through the manhole into the cistern. He had his usual piece of string, to which he had attached a safety pin, and was snagging toads out of that stagnant water about half-way down the tank. Despite the lack of good light, Bob was pretty good at this sport; but then he had a lot of time to practice, so we conceded he was the champion toad snagger. I don't know what he did with them, but I doubt if they are good eating. I was afraid to ask him, I didn't want to know!

Immediately upon gathering at the cistern with Bob, we began to press him for details about this special party. Bob, despite the fact he was presumed to be the host, didn't know any more about the situation than we did. All he knew was that he was told to go outside and play and that the rest of his buddies would be coming over for a party. That was all—period. The mystery remained unsolved.

At this time I want to point out that Bob's mom was famous among us for her mouth-watering doughnuts! It was not uncommon for anyone of us to pretend he had a sore throat or fever so he could go to Bob's house for a pill and, hopefully, enjoy one of her hot sugar doughnuts. When we smelled that delicious doughnut aroma coming from her kitchen, any undue suspicions evaporated. We were all ready for this stag party to start, and we didn't have to share any of those scrumptious doughnuts with any silly girls either! Hey, stag parties might be the coming thing.

In short order we were all summoned to come into the

house; the party was about to start. No urging necessary here, there was a stampede for the kitchen door. We were cheerily greeted by that sweet loving and kindly producer of sugar doughnuts and another neighbor lady who was evidently there to assist with the serving. We were all steered into the front room. Now this was special, since in those days, the front living room was usually saved for wakes, weddings, adults' parties and holiday feasts. What the heck, it was obvious by now that stag parties were something special, so let's get on with the party!

When we were all seated about the room, our lady hosts explained a little bit about stag parties. In the sweetest and most believable manner you can imagine, these dear ladies explained that all our parents had talked it over and had decided that now that we were reaching manhood, smoking real Bull Durham, under proper supervision, was perfectly okay. In celebration of this turning point in our male lives, they had conjured up this stag party to usher in that stage of our up-bringing.

So, these sweet ladies, whom we trusted explicitly, explained how this process worked. They pulled out a big tray of the most beautiful smoking stuff you ever saw. There were Bull Durham sacks, there was Prince Albert for that array of pipes. There were even a couple of packs of those tailor-mades. I even recall there were a couple of cans of snoose. Gosh, All Friday! It was eye popping. Oh, and did I mention they brought out some grape wine with which to wash everything down?

Until now our gang had rolled our own out of brown store paper, with finger sized corn silk fill or some knick-knick. Every once in a while one of the guys would swipe a half sack of their dad's Bull Durham. Since neither our Dad or Mom smoked, Kenny and I couldn't contribute much to that creek bank activity with the other guys, but we could gather the corn silk or knick-knick.

I also want to point out that Bill Clinton didn't invent that "non-inhaling" technique. I had learned very early on that inhaling just was not my thing. I didn't want to let on to the rest of the gang that I was only pretending, but "puff and blow" was the best I could accomplish. Kenny was the gang ring leader because he was bigger, tougher and could really inhale in great fashion, and he usually handled the "roll your own" duties. So, to this chore he stepped forward boldly, grabbing that first Bull Durham sack and some real genuine papers and the party got underway.

Actually, I was glad the other guys didn't know about my non-smoking abilities, for fear I might not have been invited to this party. I might be able to fake this puffing stuff, but sure as heck I didn't want to miss out on those doughnuts. Since Bob's mom explained that a real stag party required that the doughnuts, accompanied with those fresh picked, ripe strawberries, smothered in thick cream, must be enjoyed together, I too, accepted one of Kenny's home-rolled Bull Durham cigarettes. I lit up and "puffed and blew." No one really noticed, or if they did, they didn't call my bluff, and I dug into that pile of hot sugar doughnuts and wolfed down two bowls of berries and cream. Man, they were great!

Our lovable and sweet lady hosts hovered about us, making sure the pipes were full, cigarettes lit and, oh yes, they even produced a few cigars for the discriminating smoker. Kenny had to try one of those, for sure, so several of the other guys also followed suit. Smoke filled the room. By now, even though I was faking that inhalation, I was learning first-hand about second-hand smoke. Not being good at this smoking exercise anyway, I soon found myself feeling a bit woozy, but not the rest of the gang. This party was heady for them too, but not like it was for me. When I wanted to go outside for a bit with my doughnut and berries, I was kindly informed that leaving a stag party while in progress just wasn't acceptable.

I have often wondered over the years since then, if my being the runt of the litter couldn't be traced back to that stag party? Under today's rules, I could probably get some two-bit lawyer to take the case and sue for a small fortune. But this is now and that was then; and, after all, hadn't my legal guardians, those loving, caring and trusted parents, had a hand in this too?

As I thought about this whole event later, I just could not

believe that sweet protective mother of mine could do this to me! That same mom who nursed me through all those childhood illnesses, stayed up all night when I was distressed, bandaged my scrapes, stood up for me when Dad was sure I needed a spanking. How could such a wonderful person turn on me like that? I trusted her and Dad. Surely they must have known what was about to happen to me. By now, I was so sick, yeah man, I was willing to admit it. I was mighty sick. If I didn't get out of that nice lady's front room, there was going to be something spilled on that carpet! I rushed for the door, leaving the doughnuts, berries and cream and Bull Durham for the rest of them.

I sat out there on the shady side of the house trying to stop that elm tree from spinning around, holding my head and trying to make some sense of all this.

One thing you can say for brother Kenny, he was the rightful leader of our gang. He was tough. He hung in there longer than anyone. He bragged later that he tried everything they had to offer, and I'm sure he did. Whatever, in the due course of time, one by one the rest of the guests, including Bob, stumbled out of the house and joined me in mutual commiseration. With their extra indulgence, they appeared to be in worse shape than I was. That didn't make me feel any better, but by then I didn't feel so all alone in my grief either. Misery does love company.

What was so totally unbelievable was the sudden attitude change of that sweet lovable mom of Bob's and that nice neighbor lady. Suddenly they turned on us. They stopped being friendly and supportive. We were sick—so what!? "Out of the house, quickly before you mess up my carpet! The party's over, it's time for you all to go home!" How could this be? This sweet and caring lady was the one who made sure we had a constant supply of cod liver oil, administered by our moms, the same caring soul who tied that asifeity bag about our necks when we had the croup. How could she now be so uncaring about our condition, when it was surely obvious to anyone that we were dying!? And there we sat, too sick to walk. By now we had all tossed up those wonderful doughnuts and berries and cream.

Surely that was proof we were in dire straights. Shouldn't she call an ambulance or something?

For that matter, where the heck were our loving parents? Now that was an honest question. Yeah, just where were Mom and Dad? Weren't we still their responsibility? Didn't they even care that we had been seriously poisoned? What was in that stuff anyway? Salt peter? Paregoric? Surely they couldn't have stooped to rat poison? Just what had we done wrong to justify all this? If Dad and Mom had a bone to pick with us, why didn't they just come right out and discuss it? Why would they throw in with such a scheme? Funny thoughts run through your mind at perilous times like this.

There we sat, not recuperating very well at all. Even Bob didn't know what to say. We sort of felt sorry for him because he had to live there and trust that sweet lady to cook him meals for years to come. It was bad enough for the rest of us to assume our parents had a part in this, but poor Bob just knew his mom had to be the ring leader in this massacre! Poor Bob. We left him there beside the house. We assume he made it inside sometime that evening. I thought I heard him say something about apologizing to the toads.

By now it was getting along towards supper time. Supper time! My gosh, what a revolting thought! Made me want to throw up all over again just thinking about it. It became evident that somehow we had to head home. Brother Kenny, being our leader, sickest or not, knew he had to get us on our feet and headed back across the creek.

Now then, we could have taken the longer way around and used the roadway and the bridge, but every step was so painful. With spinning heads and flip-flopping stomachs, we didn't think it wise to step out into that wagon traffic. Even though there may not be another wagon come by for an hour or more, we fully anticipated that quarter mile could very easily take several hours at least! Instead we headed home by the path again. We went down to the north creek bank, heading towards that 12 inch wide plank of a bridge across the creek. We stumbled along, certainly not moving as my drill sergeant in later years would have found acceptable. As struggling survivors, we did quite well, I thought—we made it to the plank.

By now the creek seemed to be a lot higher. Why I don't know, it just seemed to be much larger just like the trees were bigger and moving around. The polly-wogs, turtles and crabs seemed to understand and moved out of our way. I am sure they knew darned well that the plank just wasn't going to be anywhere wide enough. I am quite sure even the sympathetic birds stopped singing in the trees overhead. And here we were about to cross this raging stream to seek sanctuary south of there somewhere. Perhaps at our homes—if we were still wanted.

Kenny was the first. He started across the plank, but by his third step, he missed and landed in the creek—mud, muck and all. He gamely straightened up, spit out a pollywog and struggled, with as much dignity as he could muster, up the bank on the other side, collapsing beside that big tree there in the park. One by one we all took our turns crossing the creek. Some just by-passed the plank altogether and waded across. I realized I had indeed suffered less than the rest by leaving that party early, as I managed to make it clear across the plank without a mishap. There was no joy, however, in that accomplishment because it was quite evident no one really gave a damn whether I made it or not. Gloating at a time like this just didn't seem fitting. Perhaps tomorrow I might bring up the subject.

Following the rest period on the south creek bank and enhanced by the cold creek water, the safari didn't take long to recuperate and get back on our feet and head up the hill towards town.

When we arrived back at our homes, it was unbelievable. You never saw such casualness! Neither Dad nor Mom were surprised we were not taking supper. Only sister Barbara wanted to know why we looked the way we did. I'm sure it wasn't because of real concern about our health since we usually bickered a lot anyway, as sisters and brothers do. I rather think she was more upset because there was a party and she wasn't invited. How could that happen? After all, wasn't she the most charming little girl in town? And she could provide the entertainment with her tap dancing. "Why

48

wasn't I invited, too, Mom?" Mom did give a little shudder as she tried explaining to Sis what a stag party was, but Barb wasn't buying that either. For once, both Kenny and I sure as heck wished our sisters had been invited! Serve them right, by golly! Oh well, now we knew what a stag party was, just in case we ever got invited to another one someday. Another one? Why?

In visiting with the other guys in the weeks that followed, we all had to admit that family bonding was strained a bit. That's when we understood the saying, "never trust anyone over 25." In fact even Dad didn't make a big issue about those delayed chores the next day. I think we pouted around a bit and spent at least two days getting them done. To this day I can't understand why I was included in that massacre. It's evident our parents, unbeknownst to us, had knowledge that there was some creek bank amateur smoking going on. If they had really done their homework, they should have known that like Clinton, I did not inhale! Oh well, I suppose I would have felt left out like sister Barbara and acted up like she did. I can't deny that I sure did learn a lesson. I never did take up smoking, and even Kenny gave up smoking—fifty years later.

As we reflected upon this initiation into manhood, via the stag party route, I guess we should be happy our society didn't practice some of those really cruel activities like those tribes who cut, carve and mutilate!

Whatever their devious methods, our parents sure managed to convey their message—though it did take quite a while for us to trust them again.

Goodbye Old Friend

One evening after school, during the height of the dust bowl drought, I entered through the back door of the little old bank building at Norris. I must have been much quieter than usual, I am sure, because I soon realized that Dad and the old rancher at his desk hadn't heard me come in.

For some reason I hesitated in the entryway wondering when might be an appropriate moment to ask Dad what chores he had for me. It became apparent right away that things weren't just right there. Dad and his old-time friend were struggling over the loan figures. It was evident that the falling markets, the loss of crops, the hoppers and all the other problems had left Dad's old friend in an insolvent condition. In the old goose-necked lamp light, I could see the desk covered with figures, mortgage and tablet work. Then I noticed they just were not saying much. It's evident they had already been over all the alternatives, and even in that dim light I could see that they were both crying. Two big, tough, proud men crying! I was 13 years old at the time and hardly a man of the world, but I was old enough to know that I didn't belong there. What they were sharing wasn't something that needed to leave that room. I have never mentioned this to anyone until now.

I didn't know for sure what all the problem was, but I could guess. I very carefully slipped out the back door and went out back of the woodpile. Then I shed a few tears myself, for I knew very well that if something was bad enough to make my dad cry, then it must be mighty serious.

A few days later as I watched out the schoolhouse

window, I saw the old friend drive a few head of his remaining livestock into our pasture beside the school. He picked up the children from school and they all piled into their beat-up old truck. A wagon was hitched on behind loaded with a few precious items of furniture, bedding and clothes. They then headed west some place. Mom told me that evening that Dad had given them $30 out of his own pocket to help them along. We charged off the balance of his note. Some years later, when they had re-established themselves "out west," they sent Dad a payoff.

For many years Charlie Allen ran the old movie theatre in Martin, S.D. "The Allen Theatre." The price of kids tickets was 15 cents, if you had that much, if you didn't have that much he would settle for what you had. And upon occasion, he would let kids in on a vague promise to bring some money next time. I doubt if Charlie ever refused any kid to see the show. No, Charlie did not die rich, but he left many fond memories with todays 'senior' citizens.

Mount Up The Posse

The Merriman, Neb., Bank had been robbed at gun point! The bandits were last observed heading northeast in a large maroon four door sedan. The notorious 'White River Whitey' gang has struck again! Be alert, take precautions!

When Blackpipe Valley telephone party line received that message you can bet it stirred that pent-up frontier spirit and got that adrenalin churning. Now-a-days we have all these fancy communication gadgets that keep us well informed on the minute to minute activities of wars in far away places, trials in Los Angeles and the like. But truthfully that old party line telephone of the '30s wasn't all that cruddy either.

With only one line into the valley from the north and one from the south, and all phones connected to the single line, it was hard to keep any secrets. If you were pregnant or hoping to become so, you just did not discuss that subject on the party line. That is, of course, unless you had some sneaky ulterior motives. We must admit, however, there were occasions perhaps, when certain lonely or braggart citizens may have utilized the system for some imagined advantage or just to get even with someone. The potential for such activity was only limited to the caller's active imagination. They used to say that there were three good methods of communication you could depend upon: telephone, telegram or tell-a-woman. It was obvious that if you had a tell-a-woman on a party line telephone, you had the ultimate.

As I recall, the party line calling ring for the Blackpipe

State Bank in Norris was a long and two shorts. To explain this a bit for the younger generation who may question how the whole community can be on the same telephone line, it was sort of like the Morris Code, where they used a dit and a da—a long or a short buzz on that noisy dingus attached to a carrier wire. Telegraph they called it. Our party line telephone worked on the same principle, using bell rings instead of dit da. So you see the Allard family call could be two short rings, while the Harris ring might be a short and a long ring. Patnoe's call could be a long, short and a long. Putnam's, two long rings, etc. etc. All the caller had to do was spin that crank a little longer and they had a long. A little quick jerk and they had a short.

Well, back to the story, now that I have crudely educated the younger folks in-re the party line communication systems serving the valley in the '30s . . .

You see, this call came into our Blackpipe Valley on a general alarm call. A general alarm call is when the caller gives a long series of longs, no shorts, mind you, all longs! Sort of like the volunteer fire department. That was the trouble call, whereupon everyone was expected to grab the receiver off the hook and listen for the emergency message. (Of course, as explained earlier, some folks assumed that every ring was an emergency ring and rubbered in on everything, just to make sure. What the heck, if it makes them happy.)

Well, whatever, so along comes this emergency call about the sad state of affairs that had just occurred in Merriman. The Anchor Bank had indeed been robbed at gun point. And those suckers were purported to be headed for the Blackpipe area. Take action! To date, the summer had been pretty dull in the valley, so you can just imagine the excitement this opportunity presented to the residents. Man! Let's do something! What we really need here, men, is a posse! Every man to his weapons! The malaise is over! Circle the wagons! Bring the women and children to safety! Saddle the horses! Sound the alarm!

Within minutes the menfolk of the area were gathering on the main street of Norris. Well, actually we only had one street so it was easy to assemble. In Norris the parking was done in the middle of the street, and traffic flowed on each side. That left the gas pump in front of the filling station handy to get to. Some bigger towns probably had sidewalks there instead. But for Norris, it worked well and the attendant didn't have far to walk when pumping your gas. And then, too, when your car didn't start, it was much easier to hook a lariat to the front bumper and tow it to start, when parked that way. Every metropolis to its own thing, I say.

So now we have the townsmen gathering in front of the hotel/cafe as the men of the rural countryside who had received the same message were throwing up clouds of dust as they tore madly towards town to get in on the fun. Man, this was going to be more excitement then we have celebrated since Todd Jr. accidentally burned down the boys' outhouse at the school while smoking hand rolled Bull Durham during a two finger break.

Like most trips there is really much more excitement preparing for the journey than the real events that follow. About the time a sufficient body of the valley's finest brave and stalwart citizens were assembled, armed to the teeth (including a few old timers well armed, without teeth) and ready for the chase, out came Joe. Joe was rushing out of his house trying to load his shotgun on the run. That shotgun went off accidentally, tearing up the sod and missing his leading big toe by inches. You never saw such immediate alertness demonstrated before in your life. All that well armed and assembled posse hit the dirt, ducked behind cars, wagons, trucks and fence posts. Anything handy. There is no truth, however, to the rumor that Clyde ducked behind his wife. Why the heck someone hollered 'There they are!' I just don't know. But they really should not have done that. I suppose it was just an impulsive reaction to his imagination. Itchy fingers of a well armed and impatient posse just did not harmonize well right at that moment. Maybe it was sort of like crying 'fire' in a movie theatre. But, after all, Norris never had a movie theatre, so perhaps you can forgive our upbringing.

There were a few very tense moments there when all

that brave weaponry swung towards Joe, and Joe was yelling at the top of his lungs to identify himself, after which things did sort of settle down. It was good practice, however, it allowed everyone to take a deep breath, expend a little of that tenseness and recheck their weaponry, ejecting some ammunition from the chambers, returning some calm resolution to the process. I often wondered later just what Joe thought he was doing, going up against The White River Whitey's sub-machine gun and high powered rifles, with a full bore shotgun.

In short order they had four vehicles fully manned with grim, steely eyed, jaws set, resolute posse men, with gun barrels sticking out the windows, somewhat resembling a covey of motorized porcupine. Their plan of attack was to take one team in each direction from town to search out these scoundrels. North, south, east and west. Find those suckers and correct their attitudes! Let the campaign commence.

Until this moment, Ted Hill, the teenage attendant at the filling station, had been unable to get anyone to listen, but finally someone in the crowd took notice. I think it was Shuz, who was a corporal in the world war and calmer than most.

Ted hurriedly explained that just prior to all this hullabaloo he had been out on that vacant lot teaching Joe's dog, Boob, to retrieve sticks, when he observed a vehicle driving at high speed, kicking up a lot of dust, going west on the road south of town, and that it appeared to turn into the old Pat Patterson place just southeast of town. He wanted to suggest that perhaps that might be a good place to check out.

The consensus of the assembled forces was that it sure appeared to be presumptious that any scoundrel, even White River Whitey, would be stupid enough to venture that close to all this awesome firepower. But, what the heck, one squad did agree to stop by the Patterson place on their way out of town. So, abandoning the women and children to defend themselves, the posse took to the campaign. North, south, east and west. Without even one single bugle call the army took off in a cloud of hot Dakota summer dust, a horn honked, a chorus of 'Ya-hoos' and they were gone.

The squad that agreed to check out the Patterson place stopped and looked about. They checked the house, could see nothing out of the ordinary. Ted's theory forgotten, they proceeded towards their assigned perimeter. Carry on, we must persevere. Let's find those suckers! Teach them a thing or two!

From this point on, things were less than dull. The only interesting event was when one of the teams thought they had spotted the bandits' large maroon car and maneuvered for several miles to surround them for an ambush. They were happily surprised to discover they had been sneaking up on Hod and his forces. Excitement and imagination had caused them to forget that Hod's sedan was also maroon when they had all assembled on Main Street several hours before.

History records that the day unfortunately produced no gunfire, hangings or arrests. It did, however, liven up a few hours of an otherwise very dull summer. Later the bandits' car was found in a small gully north of the road between Norris and Long Valley, and a bag of coin was found at the old Patterson place. It was reported that White River Whitey, at his trial, stated that they and their car were hiding in the Patterson barn, watching that team of searchers through the cracks of the barn door—weapons loaded and drawn. Luckily for everyone, the barn was not searched.

The following day, things were pretty much back to normal in the valley. A deadly serious checker game with two observers was under way again in the barber shop, as that homemade water-cooler fan hummed in the window. Slavic's blacksmith shop across the street was busy as usual, fitting a new set of wagon tires. The horseshoe game was happily clanging the stakes on the lot between the poolhall and the blacksmith shop. The usual retired citizens were again holding court on their bench in front of the Holland General Store, chewing plug tobacco, swapping tall tales in the shade of the rough-board awning. Claude had re-racked the snooker table in the poolhall again, as he patiently awaited his daily game with the mailman from Belvidere—who was late again as usual. The only dust clouds were from a few tractors back in the fields. Joe's old dog, Boob, was retrieving sticks for Ted and keeping a watchful eye on Mrs. Jorgensen's cat on the fence post nearby.

As I sat there under our shade tree, our sleepy old dog's head in my lap, whittling away on a diamond willow stick, it occurred to me that just maybe peace and quiet weren't all that bad. After all, if we really craved excitement, we could move to Rosebud or Merriman, I suppose.

In those early and late years of our life, we can usually depend upon family members to pretty much make decisions for us. During those in-between years that Internal Revenue gladly volunteers to assume that chore.

The Emergency Recovery Act

In the '30s, I believe it was 1933, the drought was on, grasshoppers and mormon crickets were rampant and money was scarce. There was no longer any feed for the last remaining cattle, and they had to be sold. Problem was, there was no one willing to buy, because the cost of hauling them to market would eat up their value. So the government stepped in and bought these last cattle at $20 for a cow and $25 for a cow with a calf at side. They branded them with "ERA", chemical acid brand, then ran them out the back gate of the local stockyard at Norris. Once there, the next Indian family in line would whip the critters into a wild run across the flats, then kill them on site and haul away almost everything, including the paunch, etc.

It was interesting to watch, especially when the first activity after the critter was killed was to open them up and roll out the insides. Then they would cut off a chunk of the hot liver and the gall sack. Standing in a circle, they would pass that hot, raw liver around, sprinkle a few drops of gall on the edge and, with a sharp knife, they'd whack off a chunk of liver and gleefully gulp it down. They would then pass along the remaining liver and gall to the next in line. After all the ceremonies were done, the rest of the critter was butchered up and tossed into their wagon. Then they plodded off for home to make their jerky and such.

Things actually went better at Norris than some other places off the reservation. For instance, at Cody and Merriman the cattle were just driven into a pit, shot and covered up, not utilized by anyone. Hogs were also bought by the government and hauled to the Missouri River where, we were told, they were shot and tossed into the river.

We had several people who shipped livestock to the Sioux City and Omaha markets. When they followed up later to inquire why they did not receive the proceeds of their sale, they were told they still owed the railroad for freight, even after the total sales were applied.

My Indian friends, who are known for their rather dry sense of humor, said the E.R.A. brand meant, "Eat 'em Right Away," which they did. After all, without any refrigeration in those days, there was really little choice.

Those Dirty Thirties

The disbelief about events was probably the first big hurdle our people had to deal with. No one could believe that such a great, fertile, green, fantastic homeland could change so quickly. The valley was filled with people who settled here just because they had never seen such tall green grass, such great first-crop flax, all the streams and springs running full. Bountiful was the accepted way of life. We all expected it and depended on it remaining so.

Well, that just didn't seem to be the same script that greater powers than we mere mortals had in mind. One summer we were swimming and fishing in the creek past the house and the next summer it was bone dry, as were the springs that fed it. The rains never came when most needed and very long spells developed when no rain arrived at all. At one time, after a very long dry spell, I heard an older farmer remark to another with a very profound and sad voice, "You know, I had an uncle once who seen it rain!" At least those early settlers did keep their humor.

When we did get a shower, it was likely to become a savage hail storm instead. Crops planted never came up at all, or, if they did, they were immediately attacked by black clouds of grasshoppers and ground-blanketing masses of mormon crickets.

The only green thing surviving were thistles—and we had to hurry to get them before the hoppers. Our ranchers learned to cut them early, while they were green, and stomp them into stacks while tossing lots of ground salt into the process. The cattle soon learned to do quite well on this supplement. The thistles that could not be harvested soon tumbled across the landscape eventually lodging in the barbed wire fences. Then the terrible dust storms piled the topsoil into this windbreak until the cattle could just walk out of any pasture as the fence disappeared below the dirt dune.

The government eventually set up hopper poison bait stations. They mixed sawdust or bran with poison and molasses and spread this about the countryside. It was fairly effective, but this indiscriminate spreading did kill a lot of birds and livestock, too. With no feed for them and the government being the only disaster purchaser at $20 for adult cattle or $25 for a cow with calf, no one really worried about a few that died in the poisoning process. For the mormon crickets, farmers tried digging shallow ditches backed up with walls of sheet metal about two feet high. As the crickets bounced off the metal and fell into the ditch, they were sprayed with coal-oil and incinerated. This was effective where possible but so very inadequate compared to the infestation.

The hoppers were so numerous that barbed wire looked to be two inches thick. Fence posts were actually trimmed of all bark by them.

It had been so long since the prairies had rain, there was talk of removing the windshield wipers from all new car deliveries as unnecessary accessories.

I was told, by a very good source, about an event on that WPA road project south from Norris. You see, the Works Progress Administration had tried to alleviate the disaster somewhat by hiring farmers and ranchers to work on such projects as dam and road construction. Those with teams and a fresno were best off and were paid more per day than those who could only do pick and shovel work. The folks with teams would drive them to work each day with a few green thistles piled in the wagon box for their feed. This one day, while they were taking their noon hour lunch break with the workmen in the shade and the horses tied to the wagon to eat the thistles, the hoppers arrived in a cloud.

Well, sir, this fellow swore to me that when they went to get the horses to go back to work after lunch—they were gone, the thistles were gone—and the grasshoppers were playing horseshoes to see who got the wagon tongue!

Daniel II

Previously I have related to you about the accumulation of wildlife critters presented to Dad by our neighbors in the Blackpipe Valley. Among them was that large pen full of raccoons. I sure don't recall just how Dad came by all of them, but I remember we had seven adults at one time. Two of them we had had for quite some time. They were really quite playful and cuddly. The five newest ones just seemed to take their confinement with a real chip-on-the-shoulder attitude. It was an attitude which I was to become fully aware of one evening after school and for which I was not completely prepared. Considering these guests had always been well fed, I just could not understand why they had all this pent-up resentment!

Our school house was just one block away. One day at school I had bragged to my friends about our new residents and how friendly they were. After all, I surmised, with those two friendly older raccoons to show them the way, these newer five adults were going to adapt accordingly. And why not—didn't I feed them regularly? I invited my friends to stop by after school and see them.

One day, promptly at four o'clock, when school let out, our little safari headed for the large cage Dad had built for the raccoons. This was a nice spacious cage. It even had a large upright climbing tree inside. It also had a watering trough for them to wash their food. As you know, coons like to wash their food before eating it. Then there was climbing rope, feeding tanks and things like that to make their stay pleasant.

We all arrived at the scene perhaps with a little more

fanfare and chatter than our pets were used to. They became a bit excited and dashed about the cage and up their tree.

Now I'm not sure who suggested this, perhaps I did myself since I always sort of liked to show off anyway, but the next thing I knew, I was entering the cage to demonstrate my "lion taming" capabilities. Maybe it was some other stupid reason, but there I was, I had intended to leave that heavy gate latch unlocked, but one of my pals, no doubt anxious to protect the ladies present, managed to slam that lock shut. The very sound of that heavy latch seemed to trigger the worst of attitudes in our pets.

Before I knew what happened those five newest raccoons were attacking—and not in any cuddly frame of mind either! Those suckers were just plain irritated and wanted to demonstrate by conveying that impression to me immediately!

In an instant those rascals were using my legs for teeth demonstrations and clawing posts. My gallery was really impressed! You should have heard their applause—that is if you could hear anything above my screams for help!

My first reaction was to start kicking coons right, left and upwards. I must say I was doing a right credible job of it. I even yanked a couple off with my hands. Then I realized that one sneaky sucker was maneuvering for snap-grab at my crotch. Now that got my immediate attention. I reacted in the most normal fashion any male with survival instincts would—I assigned that area a very high priority and both hands rushed to cover that vulnerability. While my already short legs were getting shorter by the mouthful, I continued to drop kick those furry suckers all over the place. They told me later that my shouting and jigging were quite well harmonized, but there was no doubt my guests were tremendously impressed! I received compliments on the show for weeks afterwards. Come to think of it, doing a jig with two coons firmly attached to each leg, while clutching your crotch with both hands, and all this without any previous practice, is quite an accomplishment.

At this stage of the show, one of the more tender-hearted girls present sized up the situation, bless her, and took off on a run to alert our hired girl, Hulda, as to the emergency. Even though she missed some of the best of the demonstration, I am indebted to her for being so understanding. Meanwhile, the rest of my "friends" continued to carry on their applause, and that buddy who locked the gate continued to make sure no coons were getting out—or me for that matter!

That one sadistic raccoon just seemed determined to add a bit more gusto to this performance. He just kept circling for a grab at my crotch and I kept spinning around and around to preempt those intentions. All that spinning had further advantages. It made some of those coons who were chewing their initials onto my lower extremities a bit dizzy and eventually they fell off. Now they were clearing their heads while planning another approach.

My coveralls by now were showing definite signs of wear and tear. Today such dilapidated trousers would be right in style. But for you young folks, a word of caution, I do not recommend this method of customizing your new pants. Use a razor blade, jack knife or some such tool instead, if you must.

At this time from the gallery came a flood of interesting, but not humourous (at least not to me) comments and suggestions such as:

"Are you charging for this show?"

"Did it take you long to train them?"

"Do you do this often? Maybe I can bring my kid sister tomorrow."

"Shame on you, I'm going to tell my mother what you just said!"

"What else do you feed them?"

"I thought you told us coons don't eat things they don't wash first, did you wash your legs?"

"Boy, are you going to catch heck when your mom sees your clothes!"

"Do you suppose we can get teacher in there at recess tomorrow?"

I'm sure you understand it was inconvenient at that moment to respond to all these interesting comments while

64

all my attention was directed at this presentation by these caged rascals who seemed delighted to get their jollies by nipping at my butt. I must say, however, this experience prepared me well for later years when an army sergeant liked to do the same thing!

As I continued to scream and gandy about, I managed to work my way back to the door, but since it wasn't wise to release my crotch-clutch, I couldn't get the door open. My buddy couldn't see why he ought to open it up and inherit all my problems either. I am sure he was confident I would soon demonstrate control over the entire situation. I suppose I should appreciate such confidence, but at that moment it didn't impress me one damn bit! You know, friends like that can scar a fellow for life with a terrible inferiority complex.

I am sure that by this time this demonstration had only lasted a few perilous minutes, but it did seem more like an hour. I hope you can appreciate that.

They like to tell about your life flashing before your eyes at a time like this, but when you have led a rather sedentary life in a small town for all of seven years, a total review of those recollections sure doesn't take very long! I do recall thinking about last week's Sunday school lesson where Daniel was in that lions' den. It sure didn't help to contemplate that correlation at this moment.

By now all this noise and uproar had all the disorganized precision of a six pack of attorneys at a one car rollover! This caterwauling calliope of ring-tailed rascals had reached quite a crescendo. My input was not to be sneezed at either! Even Hulda, who was in the house, had become aware, even before my rescuer found her in the pantry churning butter. She grabbed her broom and headed out the door, knowing full well that I was in trouble—again.

You must understand that aside from those first few moments of daring when I first entered that pen, I was no longer playing to the grandstand crowd. It was most encouraging now to hear Hulda yelling her battle cry as she charged into the fray—skirts and apron flying, bonnet on the back of her neck.

You know, I'm confident to this day, that some of those

darned buddies of mine would have been content to just stand there and watch those varmints pick my bones! It's in times of crisis like that when you learn who your real friends are! Hulda was even more than that, she was a darned good cook! And none of those "friends" could cook.

By now I had kicked over the watering trough and feed bunks and as those sharp teeth were getting firmly planted, it was evident even to the gallery that this playfulness may have gone on long enough. Everyone was urging Hulda to make haste. Perhaps a squad of marines or Tom Mix would also have been appreciated, but right now we had Hulda and were darned glad of it!

Hulda, totally fearless, plowed into the fracas. Batting varmints right and left she bounced those squalling and snarling suckers off the walls and ceiling. If you have ever heard a gang fight of alley cats at midnight you might get a vague idea of the noise and confusion going on here. You know, one mad raccoon can put up one heck of a ruckus. Now then, add five or six more and you might well think you are in a ringside seat at a republican caucus! That will give you the general idea.

By now, both my legs and a few fingers were thoroughly tenderized as Hulda hastily removed their attachment to me. In darned short time, Hulda had restored a semblance of order about that pen. Those varmints knew better than to mess around with Hulda like they had with me! Up their tree they scrambled, conceding the floor to Hulda, but I swear those suckers were looking me right in the eye and smiling.

Once I was out of the cage Hulda and I sat down on the grass to let her catch her breath and to assess the situation. Hulda pulled up my trouser legs to check the damage, then she headed for the medicine chest.

It was obvious to all that the show was over, but now the critique began. The whole gallery wanted to interview me at once. I suppose I should have shown more appreciation for all this attention, but for some reason my mind was elsewhere.

"Can you do this again tomorrow for the whole

school?"

"What was that dance you were doing? I thought you told me you couldn't dance."

"Do you have to swear like that even when you don't sing and dance with them?"

"Since those two old coons don't do anything, does that mean you might get rid of them? Can I have one if Mom says it's okay?"

"Tell me, are you going to make a coonskin cap out of that crotch buzzard?"

"Dad says they are good eating. Are you going to eat them now?"

"You know, one time I saw two coons down at the creek fighting like that, but I think they were making love. Were they trying to make love to you?"

"Maybe they are hungry, do you feed them enough?"

"Boy, you sure moved fast, but they are a heck of a lot quicker, aren't they!?"

"Here comes Hulda with the iodine. Boy, I'm getting out of here before you start screaming again. I can't take any more of that!"

As Hulda surveyed the repair work she had to do on my overalls, she applied that iodine with enthusiasm. Sure enough, I sent my guests away at the top of my lungs. I couldn't help but think what would have happened to history if Daniel could have had Hulda to count on for support!

Shortly after that demonstration of sheer stupidity, those five wildest raccoons managed to dig out of that foolproof pen and escape back to the creek. Perhaps they thought we might really take Jug up on his suggestion to make stew out of them. Those two older raccoons seemed to enjoy our company and stayed with us for years until we gave them to a fellow who lived in Hot Springs.

Today as I look back over this harrowing experience, it helps me to understand my lot in life, that rut I have been in. You know, those ungrateful suckers bit the hand that fed them! This has haunted me ever since, but maybe it also helped prepare me for this profession too. Those ungrateful nippers scarred me with a cantankerous disposition, a sort of cussed demeanor only best suited for small town loan officers!

Then there is a redeeming lesson learned here also. It has benefited me often over the years. That is, to always remember to protect your vitals with both hands when you are cornered and out-numbered!

Then too, who knows, what if those raccoons had let me get away with that show-off demonstration, maybe I might have gone on to become a successful politician, or even a lawyer, or both. Then there was another lost career when that middle finger got all chewed up. That sure eliminated the field of proctology.

Isn't is interesting to note the amazing similarity of these professions I missed out on? Oh well, such is life. I guess we can't all be famous like that.

That Sweet Smell of Money

Shortly after we moved to Martin we were complimented by an old-timer rancher who arrived at our lobby with his cash stash.

It seems that for a number of years he had had no faith in banks in general and some bankers in particular. He had managed his own savings in a fashion that comforted him. He had buried his paper money in a baking powder can in the manure pile. Over the years I had heard money referred to in similar category, but his was the first time you could honestly say that money smelled accordingly.

We were honored, to say the least, after all those tough years without a bank account, that he felt we were honest and trustworthy folks, people with whom he could entrust his life savings. The can had two round wads of paper money, snugly placed one on top of the other, filling it completely.

We were surprised and happy that, after those very lean drought years, that anyone had managed to save anything, let alone this nice little stash. We went out of our way to thank him. He went out the door with the first checkbook he had ever had.

That could very well have been the end of the story were it not for the warming effect of the building heat. In short order, the aroma permeated everything. We laid it out on the counter and sprayed it with cheap perfume, but it was no use. Now we just had twice as much aroma!

By next morning the rest of the cash in our teller's drawer was also taking on similar fertilizer aroma. Nothing else would do than to package up the offending "root of all evil" and ship it in for redemption; but not before we were the brunt of numerous jokes such as, "Why did you keep the livestock security in the vault?" Some folks referred to our tellers cages as "the stalls." They would ask questions like, "Who did you have to kick the crap out of to get your money back?" or, "Did you know it smells like a very cheap cat house in here?", and on and on. We never once regretted receiving that nice deposit. We just smiled and occasionally coughed!

"Trade Currency"

In 1934 when we moved the Blackpipe to Martin at the insistence of the State Banking Department, we had to reorient ourselves to the mannerisms of the new community.

The first thing that seemed to present itself was the "trade currency" that was in circulation. We had already been acquainted with the trade tokens general stores often used, "good for fifty cents in trade at..." and other similar denominations. These were used primarily in exchange between the eggs, cream and chickens delivered to the store, reduced by the groceries taken back that day; but the "trade currency" was different.

The local liquor stores and bars had cut up those old paint covered linen roll-up window shades, the ones that were green on one side and off-white on the other. These were cut into rectangular shapes, slightly smaller than U.S. currency. The local print shop then printed the different denominations and issuers on each.

Because Martin had been without a bank for several years during those trying days of the drought, the WPA and the PWA; it was difficult for folks to make change, small as it might be, when the government checks for their work arrived. The local bars sort of set themselves up as cashiers for those government checks as well as the cream check. After putting out as much genuine coin as they felt they could spare, they issued the balance in window shade currency. Of course, they expected and generally succeeded in moving some of their merchandise for part of this.

This "trade currency" was readily accepted throughout the community in lieu of cash. We accepted it at the bank just like any other check item. At the end of each day, the bar owners would stop in at the bank to issue us their check on their account with us in exchange and took their window shade money back to be recirculated again and again. Never once did we have a problem of accounting or counterfeiting.

Works Progress Administration Outhouse

During those make-work-program days, the WPA undertook to spell relief in a most effective and direct manner. They decided to get right to the bottom of things and work their way up. If any program qualified as a relief program, this one surely met the criteria. If a family would provide them enough old used lumber for the job, the WPA guys, using a standardized set of government approved blueprints, would build, free of charge, a dandy two or three-hole outhouse. Then to guard against those gremlins of Halloween, they would attach this edifice to a substantial slab of concrete base. All one had to do was deliver it to its rightful place of honor at the end of the well-worn path and establish it over the excavation you were also to provide. Relief in its truest sense.

One day as I was walking to work, I passed the popular WPA three holer edifice located behind the M&M Bar, not far from the repair shop where Harold Pike worked. Shortly after I passed by headed towards the office, Harold, in his usual humorous fashion, stepped out in front of his shop and tossed a large rock up against the back side of the outhouse and promptly ducked back inside his shop. Out of that throne room rushed six of our village drunks, who were sharing their usual morning snack, to split the air with a number of choice expletives. A quick check of the area assured them that the only other person in sight was myself and by then I was nearly a block away! After a moment's reflection, I heard one of them say, "Man, that sucker sure can throw!"

Another time, long before environmentalists, the town

used to load up the tanks on the volunteer fire trucks with DDT spray, and starting at daybreak, work up and down the alleys of the town spraying eaves, weed patches, garbage cans and outhouses to keep down the flies. On this morning in particular, our beloved postmaster, Harold James, was working with Harold Pike when they came upon the outhouse behind one of the business places belonging to a bachelor businessman. Harold James shoved the nozzle into the half-moon and turned on a blast of 150 pound liquid mix pressurized DDT. This was followed almost instantly by a horrifying female scream and some mad thrashing noises. Out rushed a local lady, with rumpled clothes, who rushed up the alley yelling for the police. Harold, who never used a cuss word in his life, stood there red faced and all trembly. It just did not do justice to the excitement when he emitted his usual, "My, my, gracious me!" The only reason the fire department didn't get torn apart in the letters to the editor in the next issue of the *Martin Messenger* was because, upon reflection, the lady in question couldn't think of any good reason for her to be utilizing that structure so remotely located from her homestead.

"Who's Minding the Store?"

Huck and his pal, Hank, managed the local hardware store. They were good at the job, had lots of friends and, by local standards, were very successful. Everyone liked Huck and Hank, perhaps too much so.

It was hard for either of them to turn down an offer on a hot day when a cold beer was suggested by a friend. It was generally said that when Huck was "out," he was probably down at his "office"—the M&M Bar.

Now Hank recognized that Huck was the boss and owner, but he also had pretty flexible work rules. If he wanted to leave for a bit, he did so freely. If he wanted to stash a little refreshment under some inventory in the back room, that was OK also. They had an excellent relationship, you might say it was 100% or at least 80 proof!

Well, one hot, not-so-busy afternoon, Huck proceeded down to his "office" to wet his whistle with the fellows. He had hardly sucked off the suds when he heard Hank holler from the back of the bar, "Huck, who's minding the store?"

Huck's blank stare told Hank all he needed to know and he rushed back up the alley he had just traversed, into the back door of the hardware store where only one customer was patiently waiting for his friend, Hank, to sell him some nails.

Hank's friend tried to convince him that he should be entitled to some commission on the sales he made for them while he was in charge . . . Hank wasn't sure if he was being kidded or not, but they resolved the obligation with a nip from the reserve supply stashed with the binder twine . . .

Huck felt so bad about Hank's hasty retreat that he arrived shortly thereafter with a cold six pack . . . contentment reigned.

Two Falls for Lawrence, One for Claude

In the late '30s the standard menu for community entertainment was the weekly community dance. For Cody, Neb., it was the White Elephant; in Merriman, Neb., the Community Hall; in Long Valley, the dance hall; and in Martin, the Milliken Hall. I never have quite figured out which was the most popular activity, the dancing inside or the fighting outside. Perhaps neither would have survived without the other. Dancing-fighting sort of became a one-word description of the scheduled events.

Some fights were scheduled weeks in advance, each community bringing their champion and cheering section. Lest I give an impression that all these programmed events with bare knuckles were a blood bath, I want to mention that most such contests were well fortified with bootleg encouragement and a lot of shots went astray. There were no official rounds, a ring, or referee, but the crowd usually policed the fair play doctrine. When one fighter finally did give up because he was too tired or too drunk or, on occasion, conceded the fight, the event was over and everyone returned to the more humane activity of dancing.

Now, in each community there was at least one local pick-up band, who played at any and every occasion, usually with mighty small or no pay. Each group had their staunch supporters. On rare occasions, Milliken would bring in a special-treat band, such as Lawrence Welk, a struggling young fellow, with his Hotsy Totsy Boys. They were from WNAX radio station in Yankton where they played regularly and sold Master Liquid Hog Tonic and Sunshine Coffee.

Well, on one such occasion, Lawrence and his band arrived in a big old touring car, with a small two-wheeled trailer on back and a flashy bright sign painted on it to let everyone know what to expect that evening at the old dance hall. Everyone was excited. Everyone, except Claude, who had his own local band and who took immediate offense to this intruder into his private territory. No one warned Lawrence. Claude talked and prepared all afternoon for this confrontation.

Lawrence and his Hotsy Totsy Boys had hardly warmed up when Claude arrived from his office at the the Buckhorn Bar followed by his entourage of loyal supporters. Most of them had also been in serious training all afternoon and showed it.

I don't believe Lawrence was used to such organized hassling from the dance floor. After all, his training for trips West River had been sadly neglected, so how was he to understand how we did things out here?

To make the story shorter and to the point, you have to hand it to Lawrence for not falling for the invitation to go outside to discuss this territorial issue. He did sense there was a necessity here to assert his own position. Certainly he was brave but not stupid.

From this point on, it became sort of anti-climactic. Lawrence was in far better shape at the moment than Claude, and it soon became apparent Claude had far over-trained. It was about a five minute no-holds-barred "rassling" match in the middle of the floor. Lawrence two pins, Claude one. Lawrence returned to the bandstand to the jubilant cheers of the Hotsy Totsy Boys. Claude and his friends returned, with help, to the Buckhorn to carry on where they had left off.

Lawrence was always welcome in Martin. In the years that followed, he was most proud, I am sure, to list such famous places as the Aragon and Trianon on his resume. I always meant to contact him sometime and see just where in that resume he related his prowess as champion "rassler" in Bennett County, SD! After all, President Lincoln also started from such humble activities and he became almost as famous as Lawrence.

Even Claude had to admit it was the best floor show any band had brought to the Milliken Hall, short though it may have been.

High School Athletics

As I read today about the financial trials and tribulations of the modern school boards, I am reminded of how good we had it when I was in school.

The extracurricular activities consisted of the usual school plays. A few basketball games, three or four track meets and eventually a few football games were held. There being no school gym, there were also no showers or locker rooms. Most basketball games were played away from home; but, on occasion, we did play some basketball in the the Allen theatre building or the old Milliken Hall. In this dance hall building, the bow-string rafters were lower than the basketball hoops, so lay-ups were almost all the shots that succeeded. There were rare occasions, however, when a well placed loop shot over the rafter or a ricochet would produce results, delighting spectators.

Not having a school bus, trips to out-of-town events were accommodated by personal cars or Alex Olson would furnish his grain truck. He would fill the box with hay, we would dig down into this and ride. We didn't go the extreme distances like they do today, but we did travel that way to Cody, Merriman, and Gordon, Neb., and Wanblee, Pine Ridge and White River.

Upon arriving at our destination, we were afforded one 25 cent expenditure for a meal, which usually consisted of a large hot bowl of chili and a bun. When you consider the local Martin hamburger joint had a large sign painted on the outside wall which read, "Hamburgers 5 cents, 6 for 25 cents, buy them by the sack full," you realize what that would cost today!

For home games or practice there were no showers, so players brought their uniforms in their vehicle and changed in that, or town kids went home to change. The school rest rooms were at the end of the paths. The usual one-finger or two-finger signals were approved communication with the teachers. Sign in and out. Sometimes a few of the more adventurous would dare to sign out and in at the same time and keep going. Usually Professor Hardy would give them about a half hour then drive his old car up to the pool hall and retrieve them.

When it came time to try the game of football, the school board got a good buy on a bunch of used, non-matching football pants from a Chicago firm and purchased some cheap purple jerseys. Oh yes, the Chicago firm also had some old leather helmets that could be folded up and put in the hip pocket. You bought your own shoes, and there were no socks nor any blocking or shoulder pads.

The second year out we were supplied with shoulder pads and a firmer helmet but none with nose guards.

We also purchased our own jock straps, as, of course, we do today. Dick Satterlee always complained it wasn't fair because only Harry Dickinson's dad could afford to buy the jock strap. So Harry got first pick of the girls because he got to carry the ball more often. The girls liked heroes.

The shoes we bought were the high-top, black leather kind with nailed on cleats of leather. After a few weeks the leather would wear away, and the nails would sure "raise hob" with anyone on whom you might step.

Coach Vine Deloria used to tell us, "When you are running down the field and you see one of those other guys laying on the ground, and it's just as easy to step on him as over him, step on him." Since Vine was everyone's hero, it was sort of fun to do just that whenever the occasion presented itself. However, I am afraid our young green team spent more time on the ground than our adversaries, and our scores sure reflected that!

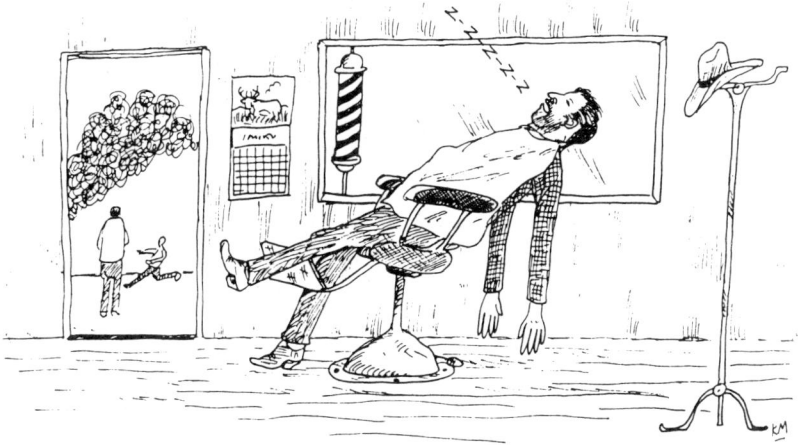

Gus's Barber Shop

Gus Jonas was one of our most active, early day fire chiefs of the Martin Fire Department. Being single, Gus always seemed to have more available time and energy and worked unceasingly for the good of the department. Gus was also our local barber. He had two chairs, but most often he ran the shop all alone. He had a wood burning hot water heater in the small back room that he kept stoked up, particularly on Saturday night. It was kept very busy with cowboys headed for the dance later. Towel and shower was 25 cents. Foo-foo water was 10 cents extra.

Whenever the fire whistle blew, it was like sticking a corncob into a large red ant hill. Volunteer firemen, racing their vehicles, and others on foot, all tried to get to the fire hall first. Whoever did get there first would drive a truck instead of having to carry a swatter or drag a hose. Meanwhile, the remaining citizens of the community, having learned from experience, scurried to a safe distance from that high speed traffic.

On such occasions, it was not unusual for Gus to have a client in the chair getting a shave or haircut. Yet, not once did anyone complain when he left them sitting there unfinished until he returned. The checker game went on, the guy in the shower left the change on the back bar and someone always stuck around to make sure the shop was locked up if Gus wasn't back yet by "going home" time.

One specific occasion, Gus was shaving a regular cowboy customer who was slightly inebriated when the call came in. Gus took off. After a little spell of waiting, the cowboy wondered why he was wasting time just sitting in this place. Not realizing he was only half shaven, he took off the sheet and crossed over to the M&M, his favorite watering hole, to fortify himself for the dance. The bartender, accustomed to the procedures here, kept him occupied and happy until he saw Gus return. He then waved to Gus to come and get his client. Gus completed the job and the cowboy never wasted a precious minute of his busy weekend.

You see, that's the sort of consumer friendly service that made small towns so close to our hearts.

Pete Swede Shoberg

There are far too many stories about this illustrious character for one short story to do him justice. Perhaps those many other stories can be covered later. For now, at least, Pete does deserve a mention here.

No one really knew very much about this tall, strong Scandinavian who came to our territory. He hauled wagon freight from the rail head at Merriman and his strength was legendary. He lived outdoors all year round and had a great fear of being cooped up by four walls. His dogs usually provided him with body warmth when he crawled into a hay stack or his wagon load of straw or hay. He had at least one horse to pull the wagon about. He usually had some rabbits, chickens and such on the wagon. Pete was an avid reader and could carry on a most enlightened conversation on almost any subject. Full bearded, with a shock of blond hair, weathered and tanned, he would do odd jobs, his meager funds were sufficient. As was his custom, Pete often camped on or near the County Fairgrounds during the winters and along the creek bottoms and timber during the summers.

One time, Pete was strolling across the prairie near the fairgrounds, deep in concentration, I am sure, when Barney came in for a landing with his old Eaglerock airplane. Neither saw the other and, sure enough, Barney managed to nail Pete to the sod with a collision to Pete's back with his lower wing—removing the wing!

They hurriedly gathered up poor Pete and hauled him to town. He was placed in the care of Mrs. Snyder, who ran the five-room hotel on Main Street. The rescuers struggled up the stairs to the second story room she prepared for Pete.

A short while later, Pete returned to consciousness. He was horrified to find himself confined in this interior environment and insisted upon gathering his clothes and checked out for the open spaces. He must have had some internal damage, but that didn't compare to the risk of indoor living.

A few years later, Pete was out strolling again, as was his custom, hands locked behind his back, headed up a side avenue towards Main Street. It was dark and, unseen, he was struck again—this time by an automobile. It was no one's fault, but this time Pete just didn't survive.

But He Kept His Eye on the Road

Van was in today. He was concerned that perhaps some of his neighbors, seeing him driving down the road to Tuthill yesterday in such an erratic manner, needed some explanation. He said some observers may have a wrong impression of the exact circumstances which caused him to be swerving about on that narrow dirt road as they passed him by yesterday. He wanted me to spread the word as to just what the fuss was all about.

It seems that Van had stopped at Cozad's feed and coal yard in Martin before heading home, where he purchased two live chickens for supper. These chickens were packaged in the usual manner, tied in a gunny sack with a binder twine slip knot. Then, for some unknown reason and to his dismay, that slip knot came undone. The chickens, sensing this trip was not in their best interest, responded in a most terrified and understandable manner. Flapping and squawking, feathers flying everywhere, they projected an honest impression that they intended to escape this situation.

Now Van's good old hunting dog had, until this moment, taken very little interest in this whole darned trip. The dog now got caught up in the excitement and responded just as he was trained to do. Corral those darned critters back into that gunny sack—and do it quick!

Van emphasized that at about this point on the road it is quite narrow and dusty. It was not the best location to have planned such an event, but in his usual best driving manner, Van dodged the traffic, skidded onto a quarter section line turn off and parked.

It was sale day in town so traffic was heavy and he was concerned that gossip would get around. He wanted it known that he wasn't "that way again," that he was cold sober and fully in control of the situation.

From this manageable location, Van now assisted Shep in rounding up the livestock and resacked them with a double knot. Of course, the happy, grinning dog was proudly taking full credit for controlling the situation.

Van just wanted everyone to know that only the dog and the chickens were celebrating.

The Launching of a Profitable Legal Career

My long-time good friend Attorney Fred Cozad likes to remind us that his illustrious career wasn't all that easy. He didn't get where he is without some adversity, and his very first case was such a foundation.

Fred had returned from his military stint, along with many of us, knowing he wanted to become a lawyer. This end he pursued with his usual energy and dedication. His magnificent success today speaks well for his early perseverance.

As you know, every lawyer has to have his first case. "We all have to start somewhere," Fred reminds us, "and you have to take what you can get until you can establish yourself."

So here we are, one fine day after weeks of trying to get a client, when a real live one stops Fred on the street asking to be represented. The gist of it being that this village drunk had once again been accosted by the local gendarmes and was ticketed to appear before the local Justice of the Peace, Judge Jake Peery, a/k/a the shoemaker, whose office was his repair shop located just north of the Courthouse.

Jake was a real historical treasure in his own right. Texas may have had Judge Roy Bean, but no one was going to take anything away from the reputation of our Judge Peery! He was a homegrown success and proud of it!

Now, at this point it might be good to explain a little more about this remarkable citizen, just so you might better appreciate some of his special attributes.

You see, Judge Jake was the envy of lots of local folks and not because of his talents with the shoe trade, but because of his eyes. Jake had two most unusual eyes, not just a pair of eyes like ordinary folks, mind you. Jake had two separate eyes, like a chameleon, you might say. Jake could fix one eye on the problem subject with all the wrath and righteous indignation of Noah, while the other eye, the noble one, would rove about the horizon to fully assess the situation.

Jake would put this talent to good use hunting grouse, too. While we ordinary folks would be squinting down the barrel on one grouse in flight, Jake would do likewise and already have that noble eye searching out his next shot. Jake was a game getter. This is not to take away any of his prowess at the checker board either. He was always one move ahead of most folks. To put it bluntly, there just was no sneaking up on Jake's blind side—he simply didn't have one.

Well, at any rate, on with the story. At the appointed hour, Fred, dressed in his Sunday-go-to-meetin' best, with his client in tow, arrived at Judge Peery's basement office/shoe repair shop, prepared to plead his first case. As they arrived, Jake, with his shoe machine running, and a shoe in hand, barely acknowledged their arrival. Finally taking notice of their presence, the Judge peered at them over his nose-end glasses and growled, "Now what do you want!?"

Whereupon Fred responded in his law school best manner, "Your honor, I am here to represent my client in this case for which he has been directed to appear before your court."

Judge Peery hitched up his suspenders to his oversized trousers. (Perhaps it is also proper to point out Jake's conservative tendencies. He always wore trousers several sizes too large for his five foot five inch, slender frame, just in case he may later put on a little weight.) Then, rolling his noble eye to acknowledge their presence, while keeping his working eye on the shoe in hand, the Judge responded, "Tell the guilty bastard to sit down, Cozad, I've got to finish this shoe first."

You might guess that at this point, Fred had a hunch this might not be an easy case to win; and he admits, the thought did cross his mind, that putting on his suit and tie might not have been necessary.

Fred has always said, "When you start out a career in this fashion, it is humbling, easy to become discouraged and may not be what they taught in college, but it is bound to get better, that's for sure!"

I like to remind folks that Fred learned well and never lost another case! I'm not sure they all believe that, but I thought that was the least I could do for a successful old friend, who had such a humble beginning.

My good friend, Dick Rose, used to delight in quoting his favorite poem:

   Dick Rose Sat Upon A Tack,

              E

          S

        O

   DICK R

Just Another Quiet Night at the Old Buckhorn

It was one of those rare, quiet, weekday nights at the Buckhorn Bar, the mellow part of the evening, when most of the folks had drifted home or elsewhere. It being quieter than usual, it was easy to pick up on the serious conversation at the other end of the bar. With nothing else really important to occupy my thoughts, I found myself "rubbering" in on this interesting dialogue.

First fellow: "Yep, I can really recommend those darned things!"

Second fellow: "You mean those little old whistles on your bumper really do scare the deer away so you don't hit 'em?"

"Yep, works like a charm. It works on dogs, too. In fact it even works on elephants!"

"Elephants! Hell, man, there aren't any elephants around here."

"See, I told you they really work! In fact, since I put them on six years ago, I have seen only one elephant. I darned near hit that one, but that was six years ago, New Year's Eve, on the way home from the Buckhorn."

"You scared it off, you say?"

"Well, actually, I had to dodge around it, but I did hit the zebra that was following."

"Zebra? Are you sure it was a zebra?"

"Yep, I'm sure all right, but the darned insurance company wouldn't pay the damage."

"They wouldn't pay? How come?"

"Well, it seems they claim that I lacked adequate

collaboration."

"Didn't you report it to the Sheriff?"

"Didn't have to. You see Clyde, the Sheriff, was in the front seat with me. But that became part of my problem, because he reported it was really a giraffe."

"So, then what happened?"

"Well, my first thought was to take them to justice court. But it happens that I also had Judge John George Day riding in the back seat, and he certified it was a crocodile! That really blew my case."

"Didn't anyone else see the accident, some reliable witness?"

"Sure enough, and that's where I thought I really had 'em. You see, we were all giving Father LaFluer a ride back to the manse at the time. He was riding in the back seat with John George. Maybe he couldn't see too clearly, since he vetoed everything everyone else had said and swore it was a rhino!"

"Surely, there must have been some physical evidence you could present to the insurance people?"

"Well, there again I thought I had 'em, 'cause Attorney Fred Cozad jumped right out of the back seat with my flashlight and carefully inspected the area. But all he could find was handful of feathers and a little manure."

"Damn, do you suppose it could have been an ostrich?"

"You know, come to think of it, those darned whistles really should be more versatile than that. Maybe I should have Attorney Cozad sue the suckers."

About that time I somehow got the feeling that the climax of this story had already come and gone and I had missed it. At any rate, with the hour now growing late and realizing there were hundreds of animals still unaccounted for, I sort of lost interest and decided to give it up and hit the sack. After all, if this did materialize into a full blown trial, the *Bennett County Booster* would keep me informed.

That's how things were at the Old Buckhorn. Some evenings were just a little more exciting than others. It does have its ups and downs.

The Touchdown Celebration

It's hard to forget that great moment in history when our struggling football team finally made our first and only touchdown! A moment of hysterical happiness and joy! We finally got one!

Overwhelmed with exuberance and excitement at this unexpected turn of events, we grabbed our coach, a rather portly fellow who was just as dumbfounded as we were, and hoisted him up on our shoulders for a victory parade to the locker room. Ted and Tom took his feet, Ed and I took the middle section and Chuck and Leo had the rest of him. We dashed madly and wildly towards the locker room to celebrate!

Dear reader, you must understand this was our first such experience, so you must forgive our lack of practice and coordination, all of which soon became obvious. We just should not have let Ted and Tom lead. They never could follow signals very well. Be that as it may, it soon became evident it was too late to change places. At a full gallop, Ted managed to clear one side of the goal post, while Tom chose the other. You can't blame the rest of us; we couldn't see where we were going.

In summation, we slammed the coach crotch-first at full speed into that darned unforgiving obstacle.

Even if we had not noticed this sudden halt to our parade ourselves, the coach was quick to call it to our attention. His screams pointed out our miscalculation immediately—if not a moment prior.

The cheering stopped immediately, replaced by some real unworldly expletives from the coach. As we eased his broken body to the sod, a hurried and unanimous decision was made by all team members to postpone the locker room celebration. Tom commented that he sure hoped the coach had his jockstrap on, for whatever good it may have done.

After all the cussing out we had endured from the coach, it just never occurred to any of us that we could feel sympathy for him; but he was so pathetic. There he lay, a crumpled, quivering, slightly paunchy piece of humanity.

Oh sure, we had heard him cuss and swear lots of times (he excelled at each), but this was different. He laid there grunting out short gasping sobs through tightly clenched teeth, interspersed with whimpers and moans, sort of like he couldn't make up his mind as to which best expressed his state of mind at the moment. We did make out that he wasn't congratulating us on that touchdown!

Joe said he thought Coach was frothing at the mouth, but since all coaches chew rollaids, I told him I'd bet it was just that. We did take notice, however, that his eyes were crossed and glazed. Actually, it was difficult to get a real clear view of the situation with him rolled up in that fetal position, legs crossed and both hands clutching the family jewels.

It became pretty obvious at that moment that Coach was not very interested in our plans for the locker room celebration. He just seemed to be out of the mood and, without hesitation, the whole team agreed. So, enmass, we all broke and ran for home still in our football outfits.

With all of his other shortcomings, Coach was always a fair fellow, and I am sure that under other circumstances, he would have complimented the whole team on our hustle as we vacated the field.

We all thought that Coach's voice was a little higher-pitched than usual all that next week. He really never spoke kindly to any of us for the rest of the season.

But Coach's wife did! She invited all of us to the drug store for a milkshake. She never did tell us whether it was for making our first touchdown or to make up for the Coach's harsh words to us. If Coach was upset with us, his wife sure wasn't 'cause she sure smiled a lot that day and the milkshakes were great!

If the Crank Doesn't Work, Push

The Blackpipe State was built on the knob that used to be the location of the most popular meeting place, the Milliken Hall. From this location it was all downhill for about three blocks, one corner included.

I always wondered if Ray Milliken didn't select that location to accommodate the jalopies of the era. After a cold late night dance, cranking that tin lizzie wasn't always easy and the demand for a kettle of hot boiling water to thaw things out wasn't always met. Very often the driver got in, those that could push, pushed, and the kids were stowed in the back under some blankets and hides. Usually after the momentum built up and the driver properly set the spark, gave it the gas and popped the clutch at the right moment everything would be copasetic.

However, occasionally, that ditch at the corner of Ray Cozad's would grab an over eager driver who wanted to cut the corner too close. If he had enough forward motion, the driver would make do with the lopsided situation until the side street one block south would toss the low wheel back onto the roadbed.

On even rarer occasions, we would observe an overly trained team head their Model T down the hill and plow it right into Ray's feed and coal yard fence. You see, they forgot who was to be the designated driver.

Shipping Time, Circa 1948

Shorty was in today to conduct his annual loan business.

He usually carried a small operating loan with us and lived on a small 160-acre place up on Bear Creek in a dugout. He is the last of those old original open range cowboys who came out west or up north from Texas to settle this West River area.

Shorty doesn't get to town often, driving his team and wagon that distance, taking the better part of a full day each way. So he needs to catch up on his socializing in this two or three day stay in town. He parks the wagon full of hay down at the livery and sleeps in the hay at night. Then, satisfied he has caught up on everything that has transpired since his last trip, he returns to the ranch.

Today Shorty was enthusiastic about his plans this fall for marketing the calf crop. I asked him what his plans were for the calves this year. After commenting upon the improved beef prices, Shorty reckoned he would take advantage of those good markets and ship the entire calf crop—both of them!

As per usual, his calves topped the local market and he was able to pay up in full again. He was also able to take home the usual winter supplies and a jag of coal from Cozad's feed and coal yard where he was a regular and trusted customer.

Along towards spring we will look forward to seeing Shorty again when it's time to plant the 40 acres of creek bottom.

John George's
Mountain Oyster Sandwich

Annually the Martin Volunteer Fire Department has had at least one fund raiser to buy equipment, fuel, etc.

One of their first and most popular was the annual Mountain Oyster fry or "Testicle Festival," as Harold James used to refer to it.

They would accumulate over 100 pounds of prepared meat, tenderize it, bread it and deep fry it. Then, they'd stuff it in a bun, spread relish over it and eat it, washing it down with a healthy supply of cold beer. The beer was supplied, free gratis by the local bars. After all, this was a popular event that brought hungry supporters to town who would usually spend the entire day in the bars building up a prodigious appetite.

One evening of this popular event, our local State's Attorney, John George, arrived a little early. The firemen had not yet had time to bring the deep fat fryers to proper temperature, but they did have the cutlets all breaded and ready to go. Well, John had skipped his breakfast and lunch preferring to utilize that time consuming an adequate amount of brew at the local pub to whet his appetite.

John showed up primed and ready, hungry as heck and allowed as how he was prepared to eat, "Where the devil was his food?" Harold Pike, never being one unprepared for any occasion, promptly and expeditiously slapped two breaded and wet oysters, uncooked into a bun and served John his plate. Harold was very solicitious and stood by while John chomped away on his sandwich. Halfway through the repast, Harold asked John how he liked them. John's reply was, "Well, they're great, but a little cold!" Whereupon still being hungry he ordered more.

Of course I wouldn't want to suggest our fire laddies served only oysters at their annual smoker. Besides the buns, they served generous helpings of deep fried onion rings, baked beans and beer. As James would reflect, it was always a roaring good festival.

There was plenty of excited conversation about plans for next year's menu. It will include a delicious boiled cabbage dish. There were also promises that next year's party will be one really big blow out.

After sixty years of banking I have concluded that there occasionally are advantages to be old, grey, short and near sighted. Most folks sense of fair play let me get away with things that people less 'endowed' wouldn't take a chance with.

HOWEVER, I learned early-on that none of these 'advantages' work with bank examineres! In fact being old, grey, short and near sighted just seems to bring out a real nasty streak in those suckers!

The Shivaree, Circa 1935

The social reporter of the *Martin Messenger* was happy to report that a good time was enjoyed by all last Friday evening at the Milliken dance hall. A Shivaree dance was held for Fizzle Smith and Dot Komm. The happy couple married quite suddenly last week. It is rumored her father had returned home, cold sober, a day early from his cattle shipping trip to Soo City and was thereupon happy to make the announcement.

At the well-attended festivities, we were entertained by the exceptional talents of the hastily arranged pick-up band. It consisted of Joe Adams on the jew's-harp, Smith Cloud was at his best on the washboard, Bull White was never better with the spoons, Andy Anderson rattled the bones with vigor, Clyde Monroe hummed the comb beautifully and Carla Schmidt whistled the melody! A truly great time was had by all.

Following the dance, the happy couple were given a wild ride astraddle the tank of our newly acquired two-wheeled chemical fire equipment. A recent fund drive by the fire laddies had provided the monies to purchase this new equipment. Unfortunately, the jostling around of the new equipment dumped the soda into the acid water and managed to trigger an unexpected discharge of the contents over the happy couple.

All was not lost. Oogatz Pudrow gladly substituted his wheelbarrow for the event, and the bridegroom pushed his lovely bride to their apartment on Pugh Street to settle in after the exciting evening.

Rumor has it some mysterious gremlins had managed to gain access to those premises and we are told the bed was short sheeted and a bit encumbered with dry cereal, syrup and a few ears of corn. We were never informed as to the tradition for the corn. We did observe, however, that the apparent rumpled appearance of their clothing next morning hinted someone had also tied some clothing in knots; otherwise, the new bride looked positively radiant!

That Warm Summer Night in 1939

It was a lovely warm summer evening with a full moon, and I was thirsty. I made my way down Main Street to the Buckhorn to enjoy a cold beer. A mad rush of excited citizens came stampeding out the swinging door like a bunch of Texas steers headed for the water hole.

Amidst the shouting and noisy activity, I managed to understand that bets were being made and everyone was speculating as to the anticipated outcome of this latest self-entertainment project. It seems Fud Dunke had just bet a quart of rot gut whiskey that he could water ski across the pond at Allen Dam on a pair of Alaskan Bearpaw snowshoes, while being towed by a lariat rope attached to Heyu Whiffle's International pickup. Everyone was headed to the main event of the evening.

I was happy later that my thirst prevailed over my curiosity and such foolishness. So I had a nice quiet hour, just myself and the bartender, to explain my theory on politicians. Then being tired, and the bartender bored, I headed home to hit the sack.

The next day I gathered a full report on last evening's activities. It seems they did get Fud straddled on the snowshoes at the south edge of the pond. And they did get the lariat across the pond to Heyu's pickup. Either the pond was too big or the rope too short so that Heyu had to back right down to the north shore of the pond. Too close. It took ten men to push him out of the mud to higher ground and better footing. A second rope was located and extended the tow.

Well, about that time Heyu's foot slipped and wedged his accelerator to the floor. That old IHC pickup let out a beller and charged up the draw yanking Fud clear across the pond and then some. The pickup took out three rods of three wire fence before it conked out on a corner post with a busted radiator. Fud's snowshoes left two swaths of ploughed sod from the north bank until the rope broke when Fud bracketed a fence post. No one thought to bring any pliers, so it took two hours to untangle Heyu and Fud and tow the pickup back to town.

By the time they all reassembled back at the Buckhorn, the bartender was so happy to see them, the drinks were on the house. I took that to mean he liked their company better than mine. I don't think anyone collected any of those bets. They were so sober when they returned no one could remember what the bets were anyway.

Winter of 1947

One very cold, blustery winter day Tuffy and I were out jump shooting the mallards along LaCreek south of town. On days like this it's a great hunt. We could see this gosh awful storm driving in from the northwest, so we decided we had best turn about and head back to the jeep we had left at the bridge. It was getting cold very fast and birds were everywhere. We must have sort of lost our concentration because when we unloaded at the jeep, we found we had a few extra birds. We always hated to waste game so we stuffed them in anyway more worried about the storm than we were about the game warden. We headed for town.

Wouldn't you know it, just as we topped the White River hill south of town, we ran into a whole line of cars, also headed to town, stuck in a big snow drift. As a further concern, who was stuck right behind the lead car, but our friendly game warden! He was on his radio calling for the highway department to send out a plow. Well, by now the blizzard was getting intense and not wanting to embarrass anyone, Tuffy jumped out during the next gust of wind and buried our excess birds in the snowbank.

As expected, we were all eventually rescued by the snow plow and went on our merry way. The next day Tuffy went out to retrieve the cache of game, and there were none to be found.

The mystery was solved, we think, when the next issue of the local news came out and a pal had a story in there about how the storm so confused some dandy mallards that he saw them fly head first into a snow bank and smother!

Surveying the Prairie Country

My good friend, Bill Hauff, aside from being an officer in World Wars I and II, the Korean War and other skirmishes and a secret service agent for the military most of his life, was a licensed surveyor.

Bill worked for a number of years between wars on a surveying contract with the Bureau of Indian Affairs, locating and charting the gravesites on the reservations. Not having a general rule or plan, graves were very often laid out in all directions, overlapping and rather helter-skelter. He enjoyed showing me some of those old maps and telling me of the problems trying to assign names to correct plots.

After Bill moved to Martin, he became County Auditor, Treasurer and performed other civic duties. In his spare time he enjoyed working on the very inadequate mapping needs of the area.

For instance, while remaking an updated map for Martin, Bill found there had been one rod length lost between the southeast corner of town and the northwest corner. This resulted in numerous minor complications, none of which, to this day, seem to be of any real concern for our folks.

When the City decided to put in a water system in the late '30s, with help from the government WPA, the rush to get that new water tower in place took precedence over sound surveying principles. After all, land was so cheap, who really cared? The result was the tower sat with two legs on city bought property and two legs on a 22 foot "lost" strip of property. This strip ran east and west adjoining what was then the lumber yard property and through the Catholic cemetery.

To correct the problem, the City located an "owner" and purchased the additional property under the two stray water tower legs. In later years Bill Porch, the owner of the "lost acreage," made a strip through the cemetery available, free, to those folks. I suppose there will always be some question as to just where the real plots are in that cemetery in relation to the surveyed burial sites.

Bill later told me his curiosity about the lost rod distance across town continued to bother him, so he began asking all the old-timers he could find about that situation. The best response he could get was that the survey was made rather hurriedly by amateurs using a cheap lariat rope cut to the right length. Then, during the course of the staking, it rained fairly hard and they assured him the rope shrunk! Bill felt there was more credibility to the story another old-timer told him. He said that as they worked their way north and west, they stopped for refreshments at the home of the local bootlegger who felt sorry for them and thought they looked thirsty.

Bill said in the early days, to survey the open range of the very cheap land, accuracy wasn't expected. They would tie a rag to one spoke of the wagon and drive in one direction for the required number of spins of the wheel as counted by the most sober man of the team. Then they would stop, drive in a tall stake with a flag on it to show the follow-up steel-corner-post crew where to dig in the permanent corner post with a marked cap. In the sandhills, where often the flag point was too low in a blow-out to be seen from the last station, they would adjourn to the nearest knob instead, so the location was more visible. As many later-day homesteaders found out, those 16 inch high steel corner posts in tall grass, located in a good driving spot, would sure raise heck with that wishbone under their Model T.

The Buckhorn Honky-Tonk

Then there was the story about Louie and Marie. They lived up on Bear Creek and only came to town on rare occasions with their team and wagon. The wagon had a little hay on board for the team. They traded eggs and cream and bought groceries. The Buckhorn Bar had a honky-tonk upstairs with only an outside stairway. They had the usual dance hall gals, a music machine and served the customers via a dumb waiter from the downstairs bar.

Louis had a bad habit of spending too long in the bar with the boys. Marie waited patiently most of the night at the wagon until the boys carried him out, tossed him in the remaining hay and Marie headed home.

One late night it was getting a little chilly. Marie got fed up and headed for the bar to fetch Louie, but at the moment Louie was upstairs visiting the ladies. Marie took a quick size up of the situation and didn't believe the boys when they told her Louie had left some time ago. She charged outside and up the stairs to the honky-tonk. Louie got the warning and dived into the dumb waiter just in time. Marie checked out the joint, then headed back down to the bar where she proceeded to join the fellows in hoisting a few. Meanwhile, Louie remained lodged in the dumb waiter, head down for a couple of hours. When Marie had had too many, the boys hauled her out to the wagon and tossed her into the back and covered her with some hay. They then hurried back to relieve Louie. By then the folks upstairs were getting might thirsty without the dumb waiter operation. Louie was too sick and weak to argue, so they hauled him out to the wagon and started them home.

It was never known just how things went at their ranch after that, but we did notice Louie didn't join the boys at the bar very often. They were surprised to see that Marie had acquired a real taste for the stuff. Thereafter, she never missed hoisting a few with the gang at the Buckhorn until they hauled her off to hit the hay. Louie waited peacefully. A few years later when Marie was arrested for husband beating, however, she did coyly admit she had known Louie was in the dumb waiter all the time. If she hadn't passed out, she would have kept him in there all night! I don't think she had any compassion for those poor folks upstairs who were getting mighty thirsty!

Where's my Calendar?
—November 4, 1987

Son Timothy came into my office to explain a bit of a problem they had out there in the lobby. It seems there was a lady demanding a new calendar for 1988, but these calendars hadn't arrived yet from the printer. She didn't seem to understand that.

I told Tim just to be patient with the lady and explain to her, one more time, that they had not arrived as yet but that we would be happy to save one for her which she could pick up on her next trip to town.

Tim went through the whole process again with this nice elderly lady but she wasn't satisfied. First she insisted he take down the old one off his office wall, a 1987 calendar. Tim explained that that was the only one he had and was using it.

The lady then asked for a 1986 calendar. Could he supply one? He explained that we don't make a practice of keeping old calendars and we just couldn't be of help to her. Once again Tim assured her that just as soon as the new 1988 calendars arrived, he would set one back for her. He then asked her again if she could wait and pick up the one he would put aside for her on her next trip to town?

Her response was, "Well, in that case, I'll just wait." And wait she did—all afternoon, until we closed the bank, at which time she quietly got up and left. Yes, she eventually did get that calendar. Now that's what you call customer loyalty!

The Home Talent Play

The Rev: Father LaFluer was the darnedest local events promoter we ever had and with no interest in profiting from it. Well, Father LaFluer decided it was time to organize a club. He called it the Martin Athletic Club—MAC, for short. At the time, the Legion was building a rough-board outdoor boxing arena across the highway from his church (where the high school is now). It was thrown together out of rough sawn pine lumber with bleachers on all sides, surrounded by a high slab wall and a boxing ring in the center. Some outdoor electric lights on posts supplied the lighting. We had some real top rated boxing cards back then and a few fighters all the way from Omaha and Sioux City. Of course, there were also the usual locally proven tough guys from Cody, Valentine and Gordon, Neb., as well as Martin. In fact, I boxed there myself at 109 pounds in the golden gloves. We also put on boxing exhibitions at the County Fair and other events.

Well, in order to promote the MAC Club, Father LaFluer decided we really needed to raise some money for promotions. He ordered a bunch of play books and invited in about ten of us as likely prospects to read and practice in his parsonage basement. He stayed with us a couple of nights to get us started, but then his "calling" to visit the boys at the Buckhorn, as was his usual practice in the evenings, required him to place us on our own while he went about his civic duties at the Buckhorn.

Things really did go fairly well for a spell without him, but in our off-stage time, some of us found it natural to wander about a bit in that large basement, while we practiced our lines, of course. At any rate, someone came across a large 55 gallon wooden barrel on a sawhorse with a spigot at the bottom front edge. That was intriguing, to say the least. Of course, I had no idea what it was, but some of the older guys were brave enough to experiment a bit. The next night and every night thereafter, we had no problems getting a full turnout and, in fact, earlier than necessary so we could read our lines before practice. Coincidentally, we each brought a tin cup.

Yep, you guessed it, three weeks went by and we were still not ready to present our play. Then one night Father LaFluer met us at the basement door with a most distraught expression and the sad announcement that future plans for MAC were being put on hold. It seems he discovered an empty container in the back room!

The Old Buckhorn Revisited

I don't know if I mentioned this before or not, but it's another of those interesting events associated with the old Buckhorn.

One evening as was often to happen, the power lines from Cecil Burd's old power plant blew down. This time it was due to a stiff wind that had caused the lines behind the Buckhorn to break and fall.

This wasn't at all unusual; hence, the Buckhorn people installed a system of old fashioned gas lights about the bar with a copper line from their propane tank. However, they did not install a light in their inside toilet, which was just a closet off the main floor with plastered cement walls and a drain groove in the floor that led outside into a pit. A person in need would just step into the room and let fly, ricochet off the walls or whatever. If you could find your apparatus where you left it last time, you really didn't need any lights. Of course, occasionally, the bartender needed to remind someone about their fly, but nothing more serious than that.

Well, back to my story. "Jug" was tending bar the night the power went off and wanted a little fresh air anyway. So when nature called, he just stepped out into that beautiful moonlit night and let fly. Unfortunately, Cecil had not yet picked up, mended his lines, nor shut off the power. Poor Jug laid that steady, healthy stream right onto that live power line! Jug told me later he never had such a sensation in his life! He couldn't move, stop or scream, although he really wanted to do all three at once! Fortunately, all good things do come to an end. When the source ran out, Jug staggered back into the bar where he immediately gulped down three cold beers. There are some of those reasonably sober witnesses present who swear that steam immediately began to emanate from Jug's fly, which he had been too preoccupied to secure. Jug did, however, restrain his dating activity for a few weeks and cut back drastically on his salt intake.

Patience may not be a Virtue but it is a Necessity

On one of Hod's field trips during the '30s, he was prompted to call upon one of his ranch loans to check on the livestock security for the directors. It was generally known locally that this fellow was having a tough time of it, and his few cattle were getting fewer. Hod and the borrower met out at the gate, and when he learned of Hod's needs, the rancher retrieved his jacket and cap and got in with Hod to drive the pasture.

Even after a careful recheck, they just could not locate a bull that should have been there. The rancher reckoned as how he must have gone astray. Since he only had ten head in the first place, this, along with the declining markets, left his loan on the ragged edge. However, being the good host, as all good ole boys were in those days, he insisted Hod stay for supper before the long drive back to town.

During the evening meal, the good ole boy just couldn't handle the guilt any longer. He admitted to Hod the family was short of food and what Hod was eating was the bull he had butchered. Faced with the reality of the situation, Hod and the rancher worked out a plan together. With Hod's support, two years later everyone was solvent again.

On another occasion, I was rewriting the livestock mortgage paper for a rancher living west of Martin. He pulled out his tally sheets and was reading off the count and breakdowns when his wife interrupted, very distraught. She said, "I can't continue like this. We don't have that many cattle any more and I just won't be party to telling you a lie. A couple of winters ago we lost a few heifers, and you guys have just been adding them back in along with the calves they would have had. Now the problem is catching up with us. Do whatever you have to do, but we do not have that many cattle any more." It was awfully quiet for awhile, she was crying and the rancher was about to start crying himself. We tossed his tally book and started over with a true count. It was overloaded, but I assured them we would stay with them, if they would hang in there, too. Sure enough, three years later, with some good crops and better markets and tight belts, they paid us off in full and retired with something left for themselves.

106

That Warm, Non-Busy Afternoon

It was a really nice summer afternoon, one of those days when all our farmers and ranchers are too busy at home to come to town on business. Jumping at the chance to get outside myself, I took off my jacket, rolled up my sleeves and, grabbing a set of trimming shears, went out to the south side of the bank and started trimming the rose bushes.

I hardly noticed when an out-of-town car parked at the curb nearby until the tourist stopped for a pleasant chat. He asked, "What are you doing, cutting down the roses?" I responded, "Yep, I sure am. I'm going to get even with that ornery sucker that runs this place."

The flustered tourist hastily left and entered the bank to conduct his business. He hurriedly informed the teller what he had learned and suggested the manager should be told right away. The teller suggested perhaps he would like to tell him, himself, as he was outside trimming the roses

The sheepish tourist did have a good sense of humor. He made sure to let me know I might be the boss, but I sure as the devil didn't know beans about trimming roses!

Halloween

As I drove along today, I spotted an old outhouse beside the road, and it brought back endearing memories of the days when such edifices were not so abandoned and forlorn!

My goodness, what happened to Halloween? What do young folks do these days for Halloween traditions? I can remember when any outhouse that avoided the usual tip-over that evening was a real exception or an engineering novelty!

Halloween was usually approached by the outhouse owners with some whimsical acceptance of "what will be will be," or "after all, boys will be boys," or even some sense of righteous understanding of "I guess I have it coming from my own younger days."

Occasionally some stubborn folks like my dad would enjoy the challenge and take firm and drastic steps to frustrate those midnight traditions. Some would sink heavy corner posts and bolt or wire them down, which didn't always work if the goblins were really dedicated to their activity and brought a team of horses or a tractor along. In fact, I suspect it may have inspired some goblins to extremes.

Dad went through those usual early years when we made sure we all went to the "can" early on Halloween, just in case it wasn't readily available at day break. Then he decided to build a large wash house, where he installed a large wood-burning cookstove. In this building we did the laundry to keep the steam and heat out of

108

the house, especially in summer. Then in a corner he dug a deep pit and built an indoor privy. Bingo! No more concern about Halloween pranks. When we moved to Martin, he continued this thinking. After we finished building the garage with a boys' bunk house in one unit, he also built the outhouse annex, attached with an outside entrance, but securely anchored to the whole darned main structure. It is still in place, but, of course, it hasn't been used in years, because shortly after building it, Martin acquired a city utility system.

I am also reminded of times when necessity or lack of concentration prompted a situation. Occasionally someone just happened to be using the outdoor facility when the tip-over crew arrived upon the scene. It wasn't too bad if it was tipped backward or sideways, although, admittedly, it was a little messy. Once in awhile, the direction of the arrival and the direction of a good tip did place the user inside in jeopardy when the unit was dumped on its face. Crawling out that user hole could be somewhat difficult as well as messy. It was not a consumer friendly situation. Of course, the expletives from inside usually prompted the tip team to make a fast and distant retreat, survival and health being uppermost in their minds.

Speaking of Halloween—it has always been an unsolved mystery to me how someone managed to put the neighbor's milk cow up in the belfry of the schoolhouse. It was only 200 yards from my bedroom window and I never heard a thing! Considering what a project it was for a crew to remove this old gal the next day, it was all the more amazing how they put her up there in the dark. All this, you understand, before power operated equipment such as fork lifts were invented. It's a fact, those gremlins in the old days did wondrous things when they put their minds to it!

The gremlins weren't the only wondrous performers involved in this incident. Have you ever watched a cow, who hasn't had much sleep, being milked in a belfry?

My Visit with Flash Johnson

Flash has always been a quiet sort of fellow. Some folks took that to imply he wasn't as bright as they were, which just goes to show how wrong they were. Flash was just not the talkative type. He was a conservative who practiced his own thoughtful conclusions.

One day when Flash was in he surprised me when he volunteered some friendly chit-chat about things at home and his wife, Flo. Since this was so out of the ordinary, I encouraged him to stay and visit a bit. After we covered the crops, the cow with twins, the new outhouse and the garden, he went out of his way to give special commendation to Flo's part in all this success.

I then asked Flash how long they had been married—38 years! "Gee, that's great," I said. "To what do you owe this long happy arrangement?"

"Well," Flash said, "we very seldom have a fight. We have a little tiff once in awhile, but when that happens, we have a sure cure for that and carry on."

"Sure cure?"

"Well, yes. You see, whenever she yells back at me, we drop the subject and we don't talk to each other until we cool down a bit."

"So how long does that take, usually, Flash, before you converse again?"

"Well, sometimes it takes six or eight months, sometimes less. It depends."

"Six or eight months? My gosh, Flash, that's a long time, isn't it? Doesn't that raise heck with your love life?"

"Hell no! We always talk plenty when we have sex!"

"But, Flash, you just said that sometimes you don't speak for six or eight months! That must get a little tense. Surely there must be times when it's not that long between arguments and that stuff.

What's the shortest time between arguments?"

"Well, let's see. This is the tenth of July. I guess that makes it about six weeks and four days so far."

"You mean, Flash, that it's been six weeks and four days since you and Flo enjoyed a little lovemaking, is that what you're saying, Flash?"

"Yep, that's the way things are. That's why we have such a successful marriage!"

"Well, I'll be darned. By the way, Flash, how many children do you have?"

"One, a girl—she's 37 now. Lives in Rapid City. Married to one of those windy liberal lawyers! I've got nine grandkids!"

"Guess that figures, Flash. By the way, I suppose she favors her mother?"

"Yep, she does."

"You could crawl under a rug to hide from some bureaucrats but then how can you avoid the one they hired to stomp out the bumps?"

The Lay Away Plan

Our morning coffee session is a mighty important part of our rural social life. This divulgence is nothing new to any small town. I insert this information so that other folks might better understand us rural folks. We take this activity mighty serious, you see, and when we lose that routine from our daily lives, even for a few days, we really miss it. So when we lost that privilege for six weeks, that was a real calamity. Here's what happened to our coffee gang one time.

Zig, the friendly undertaker, and I met our pals, Stud and Toad, that morning at the corner hamburger joint for coffee. Actually Stud and Toad sort of referred to it as a brunch since they had already indulged in a morning repast of pig knuckles and a six pack of beer. They were only sharing their company with Zig and me so that we wouldn't think they had forgotten us. The fact that Stud's new bride was waiting tables there might have had something to do with their presence. Well, whatever, there we were, swapping the usual tall tales and gossip. It was only natural, of course, that Stud and his bride were catching some good-natured kidding about their puny appearance since they had only been married a few days.

The next thing you know, Stud is asked what he intends to do with that dandy new Sunday-go-to-meetin' suit he bought for the wedding, since everyone knew he was by nature a sweatshirt and blue jeans character. Well, sir, one thing led to another, and the next thing you know, Toad suggests that Stud be laid out in one of Zig's caskets in that outfit and have his picture taken. Just to see what an impressive cadaver he might make. Just in case this married life was too much for him!

In no time at all there we were at Zig's establishment with Stud dressed up in his wedding outfit. Stud stretched out in the casket. Toad crawled up on Zig's step ladder with his camera to get a good angle for the portrait. Zig made a few last minute

112

professional touchups and adjustments. I held a drop cord spotlight. Everything was in order, except that Stud had a problem keeping a straight face and was giggling outlandishly while Toad was telling him to straighten out and shut up.

Until this point, this project was moving along in a rather orderly fashion, for a bunch of amateurs, that is. Then things just sort of unraveled and went all to hell.

First off, the local fire siren went off. Zig and I being volunteer firemen felt it our duty to run outside to see what the situation was. We had no more than cracked open the door when Stud's mongrel dog, Stud Too, dashed between Zig's legs into the funeral parlor and made a dive for Stud, all laid out in that casket. In that endeavor Stud Too managed to upset the step ladder and Toad, swearing loudly, crashed down upon the casket, slamming the lid shut.

By the time Toad had picked himself and his ruined camera off the floor, there were heard these horrible screams and dog howls coming from the casket. It was clearly an uncomfortable place these two Studs found themselves. They were making every attempt to convey that message to the outside world.

With Toad back on his feet again and no longer worrying about a replacement for the camera, he sensed Stud wanted him to pay some attention to his situation. He was happy to address that need, but how was an untrained cowboy like himself to know how to open these darned things? Weren't they supposed to stay shut when properly used? The screams, muffled as they were, continued. So Toad tore out the door looking for Zig and me. We hadn't had much time to travel anyway, so he located us within a block. Measuring the priorities here, Skippy's out-house fire or rescue the Studs, Zig's decision was an easy one.

Back we came on a dead run. Even for Zig, this was a first. He had never had to open up for a live one before. But like the true professional he always was, he had that lid up almost before Stud turned a light shade of blue! Stud Too, out of sheer panic, had a firm grip on Stud's groin.

If for one minute this problem could have been foreseen, we would have made some changes in plans. First off, we would have trimmed Stud's toe nails; that for sure was a priority. Then, too, we wouldn't have let Stud Too in that door. Lastly, Stud would not have had all that beer and pig knuckles for breakfast!

It wasn't so bad that the suit was done for. Stud probably wouldn't have gone to church in it anyway, and he wasn't about to get married again in the near future. But how any two animals could shred all that beautiful silk lining in such a short time was amazing! The further problem created with Stud's upchuck, topped off with the dog's fragrant contributions of expression, really made a mess of that dandy new casket!

By now Zig thought this fun had gone far enough and he demanded all of us to share in the damages. Obviously chastised and somber by this time, we all dug down and gave Zig what we had. It still took Zig ten days to clean up the mess. I don't know whether to believe it or not, but he said he also had to include that casket in one of his discount arrangements to move the merchandise.

Most folks would agree we had suffered enough from this ricochet project, but when Stud's wife shut us all off from our morning coffee until he recovered his potency, that was pretty serious. We fed him raw eggs, mountain oysters and bought him armloads of girly magazines, but it was slow going. Did you ever go six weeks without your morning coffee? And that bride remained adamant, if she had to abstain, then we would, too. Don't ever try to figure out a woman!

I am quite sure that most non-bankers would be amazed at the number of folks, who, after withdrawing more money from their account than they put in, are perfectly content to discontinue business with you, because you are so careless!

An Enlightening Experience

A good friend stopped me the other day to say that he had read my previous rendition about the restroom facilities (or the lack thereof), at the old Buckhorn Bar. First, making me promise not to divulge this source, he related one of his own first hand experiences, many years ago in that same facility. Obviously it was a most impressionable moment in his young life, as he remembered every detail quite vividly, with gestures.

As you may recall, I mentioned that the restroom at the Old Buckhorn was a door off the main barroom into a closetlike room, cement plastered walls and floor with a drain ditch at the back wall to catch the accumulations, whereupon it drained outside into a cesspool. At the time that I told you about in that first story, this room did not have a light inside, after all, electricity was very undependable, and using their gas lights was deemed to pose a possible serious hazard, perhaps not. Not being an expert on explosives, the management just chose not to gas light it—why take the risk when everyone is having fun?

Well, my friend now tells me that soon after that first event I told you about, the management did, in fact, install a drop light, bare bulb fixture, with pull chain in that most essential facility.

At the height of the revelry of the evening, my friend left half of his fourth beer on the bar and hastened to use the facility. You know, we have all been in a hurry on occasions like that, so it's understandable that by the time the door closed he had the zipper down and a good flow in progress.

Suddenly realizing that there was now a light available, why not use it? He reached upwards in the dark for the pull chain. Now it seems that some nefarious cuss, needing a bulb at home or with a serious mean streak, or maybe he just couldn't stand the sight of himself. But whatever the reason, the bulb was missing. As my friend completed the live circuit with his thumb in the empty socket hole all sorts of exciting things took place. He swears that blue flashing lights bounced from wall to wall with him as its source. Smoke filled the air. His eyes crossed and his hair looked like a $2.00 marcel! It seemed to him that it took forever to deliver those three beers. His insides took on that well done feeling! Finally, weak, sweaty and trembling it was over, he staggered back into the bar where everyone excitedly asked him what the flashing lights were all about. They begged for a replay. It took two glasses of cold beer to cool off the zipper, whereupon the barmaid with a pair of pliers and a bung starter managed to get it to close up. His hands shook, he spilled the next two beers his body was craving badlly. If some prankster about then had shown him a bare light bulb he would have been dead meat!

My friend summed it all up by swearing that the whole affair was a most enlightening experience. A shining moment in his life! If a restroom is dark when he gets there, that's fine with him, he sound shoots.

You know, I really hadn't noticed it before, but as he walked away, I realized he sort of walks a little hunkered over. I have always believed everything he told me, but that's just further proof as to his veracity.

I still won't tell you his name, but if you just happen to notice a hunkered-up old duffer, who won't turn on the restroom light, you may be getting close.

Reservation Time

Letter to the Editor

I want to take this opportunity to inform the peoples and correct them mis-information rumor thing that goes around about the res . . .

You don't have to have a college degree to know that just cause the WaSicu uses that calendar they brought with them from Europe, when them peoples invaded us, to know that there are other races of peoples who have their own way of telling time . . . Take those yellow people for instance, they don't give a yen for that white man's calendar . . . And I remind all you Red Man brothers that just cause we don't take a big issue with those government people what date is on check of month of December or tell them it is really Month of the Popping Trees . . . There is nothing to be gained by arguing with the great white father, but we all know, don't we, that there is white man's government time and then there is reservation time . . . Our time! That is traditional time . . . We don't need those Timex and Big Bend or Mickey Mouse watches to tell us what to do . . . Ennit?

So now that I have stipulated those sacred and traditional rights about time, I will now answer those complaints from some people who say that our Committee for Environmental Evaluation and Grant Supervision, have been neglectful in our regular meeting duties . . . I say to you, that this is not so . . . Those meetings were called, as you know, to be held in locations of most convenience for members thereof, and such called meetings were stipulated to be conducted with proper quorum at SRT hours. (Standard Reservation Time) . . .

Since I am the secretary and treasurer of that duly appointed organization, I feel it my sacred duty to instruct everyone that it'is not so, that we have failed those duties, that we did hold said meetings and I will tell them to you at this time, from memos that I have in my possession as stipulated to be as follows . . .

First I tell you that meeting called for October 10, to convene at the round house could not take official action with them grant monies, because we did not have a quorum of four peoples . . . Charlie, Andy and Me (Donn), got there that day, but John and Clyde, they had a basketball trip to the City and Clara, Enoch and Ted were drawing commodities . . . Some motion was made that we postpone meeting until next week sometime whenever next commodity truck arrives, and conduct such affairs at Commodity shelter . . .

Well, that commodities truck she never showed up at all that next week, due to usual government mismanagement and waste . . . So when word got out only two board members came to meeting location place . . . I made a note to that affect . . . So that I tell you.

Charlie said that lets try to meet at Whiteclay on next Tuesday . . . So I properly noted to the membership . . . Three of us waited all day at the Whiteclay tavern, until fourth membership showed up, but by then we lost Ted, who was sound asleep in booth four and we could not wake him for official duties . . . And he had not endowed anyone present with proxy . . .

Since there was an All Indian tournament scheduled for the following week in Rapid City, a move was made that we set next meeting date to be located conveniently for most everyones, at Scenic Bar, which would be easy and convenient place to stop at for everyone . . .

Some board members left for the City earlier than others, because them kids played in earlier match . . . So by time a quorum arrived on that scene, those early members had to leave for that emergency to Rapid City game. But me and Clyde and Clara, we stayed most of the day . . . Until Ted he came late . . . Unfortunately we had not got a proxy from Clyde this time, and he was asleep in the sawdust . . . I hear that someone did stole them boots of Clyde after we left for that Rapid City . . . I so memoed this and wrote that down officially on that Budweiser napkin for the official records, that I can show anyone, officially.

On the road to Rapid City, Clara told me, "Why don't we schedule next official meeting to be conducted at the post office, on November 3, that check day?" So, mentioned by that member, Clara, I so officially notified all those members thereof to next meeting, November 3, at the post office SRT . . .

You all know about them bad storm day, November 3. No quorum until Tribal Patrol car showed up with John, we asked them patrolmans for a stay of execution delivery time for John to appear, and we officially conducted that regular meeting for that Committee for Environmental Evaluation and Grant Supervision at them hours of 3:00 p.m. Reservation Standard Time . . . Bills were allowed and paid for the refreshments used at that Whiteclay and Scenic bar convention meeting rooms . . . And for benefit of rest of you citizens who have inquiry about them grant funds checks, we are assure you citizens that them checks are in the mail, so now you don't need to complain to us board members any more about them checks.

Officially signed by Me,

Donn Keeooti

Secretary and Treasurer for the Official
Committee for Environmental Evaluation
and Grant Supervision

Dated this 8th Day of December, 1997 SRT

Revisiting the Buckhorn Bar, Again

To say the regular clientele of the Buckhorn were playful folks doesn't quite cover their talents. They were also sporting, inventive and entertaining. I remember arriving one evening just in time for the final showdown of the "bet of the evening." It seems there had been a lot of good natured bragging about the urination prowess of the boys and gals assembled. As the beer flowed, the bragging grew. It seems one gal, in particular, asserted that, despite some obvious differences in equipment, she could, with proper preparation, out distance the prowess of any man or boy present! In fact, she insisted she could project a good, clear, solid stream over the bartender's new Lincoln parked out front! Bets were laid, beer was consumed, and now was the time for a showdown, or should we say show up? Whatever...

Everyone piled out front. It was around midnight and fairly quiet on Main Street except for those involved in the contest. I am sure most of the bystanders couldn't care less who won. Either way, it was too historic an event to miss. They would never forgive themselves later, if they missed this one.

The lady in question studied the distance from the left fender, checked for the wind, moved a little more to the rear. Then quickly preparing the equipment with a firm right-handed grip, let out a wild yell and let fly. And fly it did! Talk about an astonished gallery! She cleared the top of that new Lincoln by 18 inches at least. A yell went up from the crowd! There was hardly a dry eye in sight! (The wind was quite gusty, did I mention that?) Of course, some folks are never satisfied and wanted to make their bets a two-out-of-three deal, but there were enough fair-minded supporters who stuck by her and insisted she had won fair and square.

Being the big winner, the little gal then offered to buy the beer for everyone. Whereupon the gallery re-assembled inside for polish sausage, pretzels and beer. But the management would have no part of her money, it was all on the house!

That's one thing you could always say about the Buckhorn. It was one of those classy joints that sincerely believed in quality floor shows and cost was no object.

Let's Celebrate

Martin Luther King Day

Martin Luther King Holiday, 10:30 a.m., January 20, 1986

Clusie Ann came in today with her young daughter. I would say she was approximately three years old. The little gal was arguing with her mother that it was too hot in there. It seems Mom really wasn't paying much attention, since she was in an intense conversation with Dode at the teller window.

The next thing that caught my eye as I looked out over the lobby was a coat flying through the air. This was followed shortly thereafter by a flying sweater. Then up flew an undershirt. By now I was a little curious, so I stood up to see what was going on. Standing there in the middle of the lobby was this cute little gal struggling with her pants. She had them half off before her mom sensed something was wrong and put the clothes back on her. Clusie Ann went back to her business conversation.

Mom underestimated the dedication of her daughter. She went right back to the project, tossing clothing items everywhere. Only this time she was making better time. In a very short while she was stripped naked except for her shoes!

When she began laughing gleefully and streaked off across the lobby, her red-faced mom rushed over to reassemble the ensemble and hurry out. We've had strikers before and picketers out front, but this was our first full-fledged stripper.

I don't know if the excitement of Martin Luther King's birthday had anything to do with this, but should stripping on his birthday become a tradition, I am sure the day will become an unusually popular holiday! And at my age, I am afraid to advocate for that. After all, remember, January gets sort of chilly sometimes.

If You Want To Be Lazy, Progress

As these years roll by and I find myself standing at the section line crossroads while the new generation roars by in a cloud of dust, I find it somewhat consoling to fall back on reflections . . . Surely this isn't the first time that old timers such as I have become, have felt left out of the current levity of events . . .

There I stand . . . Totally adept at telling the grandkids all about those good (or bad) old days, depending upon the lesson subject matter I am about to expound upon . . . Confident of course that not one of them are old enough to point out any small discrepancies or liberties I interject . . . Yet, as I stand there, I get this sad feeling of inadequacy, for both the grandkids and I, know that I don't know beans about these new-fangled gadgets they refer to as a computer . . . Yet my three-year-old grandson can make them hum . . .

As this sadness of inadequacy decends upon me, I retreat into this soliloquy seeking some reasonable, justifiable excuse for this situation . . . And that's when I find solace in remembering back a few years when our parents, and their parents, must have suffered the same pangs . . . We all know of course, that progress is just simply the result of pure laziness! . . . Sure, ask any elder generation . . . The children just don't appreciate doing the chores like Dad has all his life! Just because it has worked quite well, is no darned reason why we, the new generation, can't find some shortcuts and reduce some of that hot, sweaty, physical endeavor . . . What the heck, if we can come up with a gadget or a whatsit that will get the same job done, in half the time, then we will have that much time left over to enjoy the good life! . . . And, complain as we elders may do, that trend is never going to change . . . Granddad couldn't get all the chores done on his 160 acre homestead, working long hours, seven days a week . . . And here we are now, reading abut arguments concerning four days a week . . . More time is needed to play with those expensive toys we have acquired . . . And, as has happened for thousands of years, we elders profoundly and emphatically predict that this new generation is destined "to go to hell in a hand basket!" . . . "Just you mark my words" . . . Who the heck wants to mark those words, obviously just another elderly nut, who is as lost at the crossroads as I am, and neither of us will be around to see if that prediction comes true anyway . . .

At any rate, I do get some comfort in knowing now, how Dad felt whenever I wanted to interject some new, labor saving, process into the business . . . He would shake his head, mumble something about "why change something that has worked well all these years," but he let us youngun's give it a try . . . That's not to say that he didn't still stick with his old hand tools which he loved to apply to his woodworking projects . . . Keeping them clean and sharp . . . And within that small private hobby-world he enjoyed in his spare time, he allowed no deviation from his tried and true methods . . . I recall the time that someone of the family, feeling sorry about him whaling away for hours at his lumber pile with his trusty (and sharp) handsaw, presented him with a electric power saw that would accomplish that chore in minutes, instead of all afternoon . . . And, in typical Dad fashion, the 'darned thing' got lost in that orderly tool shed and never did get the opportunity to prove its true capability . . .

Then, too, I recall Dad telling about his Dad, who very reluctantly in his later years, was talked into hanging up the buggy harness and buying one of those new fangled model T's . . . Never being happy with the fact that "Whoa, damn it", just didn't save those gates or the back wall of the barn . .

And then, I recall Dad, in his later years, purchased an over-powered new Oldsmobile, loaded . . . He drove it home, proudly, much too fast, dived it into the garage, leaving a beautifully clear imprint of the front bumper on the back wall . . . Then getting out to come into the house to complain that that sucker was "going crazy out there" . . . We went out to find that somehow lights were flashing, buzzers buzzing and all sorts of disturbing reminders like that . . . He hadn't closed one door completely . . . The four-way flasher had become active (and for that matter, maybe he drove it home that way) . . . It seems that these things just seemed to encourage every other red light and noise maker to get into the act! Of course, we 'very smart' younger generation, had no trouble locating the problem and impressing Dad with our superior knowledge! . . . I know that Dad was just tolerating us, he would much prefer to have his old car back instead! . . . And, after all, if it hadn't been for this new generation messing up a good thing, these new fangled inventions wouldn't be out there to complicate our lives . . .

I have to admit here, that when we purchased our last new auto, all this came back to mind . . . Because for some reason, we couldn't get the darned radio to come on properly . . . (And just try and buy a car anymore without a radio, they think it's a necessity, but darned well list it separately as an added accessory) . . . Well, a return trip to the dealer and his young son fixed us right up . . . Very discreetly never mentioning, even under his breath, about our generation . . . He just poked the right buttons and bingo . . . It worked perfectly . . .

Which not only humbled me somewhat, but helped me to understand a similar event that soon followed, involving that same dealer . . .

Another older generation, very dear friend of my Dad's, had also purchased a new pickup . . . Loaded, just like dealers prefer to deliver these days . . .

So our friend takes delivery and drove home . . . hitting that traditional mudhole on the way. To find that windshield wiper switch required a short pull over to the shoulder of the road . . . Sure enough, it was located and turned on full blast, the washer also kicked in . . . "This was one slick outfit believe me" . . . He turned off the wiper, and proceeded on home . . . Only to discover to his concern that every so often that darned wiper would kick back on, do a 'swish-swish then shut down again . . . Nothing too serious when you consider what a beautiful, expensive hunk of metal this thing really was . . . But next trip to town he would have to call this to the attention of the dealer . . . And sure enough, next trip to town, the same young fellow explained that instead of those old fashioned, one-speed wipers we had all become adjusted to, this sucker was a variable speed doodad . . . He thought that he had covered the instructions fully . . . But you know, just like I have a problem when my grandson tries to give me the basics of computers, sometimes it doesn't soak in . . .

Sure enough, not long after that, the darned wiper didn't get fully turned off, and the 'swish-swish' again became a distraction to our friend . . . So when he crawled into the cab of that new outfit in front of the Co-op station, and started up the motor, and that wiper kicked in, and he was grabbing for the switch to stop it, his foot slipped off the brake, caught the foot feed, and that brand new sucker rocketed across the street, jumping two curbs, in reverse, and buried itself, box and half the cab under a new semi-truck that had the misfortune of parking a few minutes before directly in that target zone . . .

Thankfully, our good friend was leaning forward looking for switches, so he wasn't badly injured . . . There he was, face and steering wheel, both straining to see who could get closest to the windshield, the motor smoking, a cloud of dust, a gathering crowd of concerned citizens, and the windshield wipers going 'swish-swish' . . . 'swish-swish' . . .

So now you see, knowing what my elders had to go through, I take consolation in my own situation, and I don't really feel so bad that I'm still standing here at the cross roads . . . I take a solace in what I have grown comfortable with. I'll just get off here, I'm sure that my kids and grandkids will look out for my interests farther down the trail . . .

Exercise is Great

My friend Fred insists that there is nothing better for the soul than that brisk, early morning jog. He wastes no opportunity to praise the virtues thereof. He met his match, however, when he tried to convert Wes. Wes assured Fred he got all the exercise he needed being pallbearer for his old jogging friends.

This brings to mind the philosophy of Enoch. Enoch tells me he also has a lot of good friends who love to golf. The pressure is constant as to why he should join their group of avid pasture pool-shooters. Enoch has his own back-up study on the subject:

1. Those fellows walk about two miles in two hours before they can enjoy that 19th hole refreshment; whereas, for less money than green fees, he could spend those two hours at the pub and be way ahead of those guys.

2. He doesn't worry about the weather interfering with that activity. Thunder, lightning, rain, snow or sleet, he is always comfortable, day or night, at his pub stool.

3. He insists the profanity is much more respectable in the pub.

4. If he really decided to take up walking, he is confident he could straighten out those same miles they walk and see the world instead.

However, bowing to pressure from Fred, family and the doctor and accepting that mid-life has produced some mid-section expansion that perhaps should be addressed, I agreed to do some evening walks in the countryside. We established a regular routine. My good wife would drop me off on a side road, two miles outside of town and I would head home. Whereupon, sure enough, along would come a good friend who, feeling sorry for the fat old man, would insist upon giving me a lift back to town. Although, I must admit, once or twice some anti-banker drivers did put me over the barbed wire fence. Well, whatever, those free rides worked great until one time no one came along at all and that walk darned near killed me!

Superla

During my stint in the army I spent most of the enlistment in the quartermaster supply. It was always busy and interesting, a real treat compared to what so many of my buddies had to endure.

On one occasion, while stationed at Fort Brady on the Michigan/Canadian border, we had a large contingent of varied troops doing guard duty over the famous Sault Locks through which it was absolutely necessary we ship the steel for the war effort. There were Navy, Coast Guard, Air Force, anti-aircraft artillery, barrage balloon battalions, infantry and the usual service groups. The countryside in the summer was heavily infested with a jillion hungry mosquitoes with which we had to deal.

To handle the situation, they provided our quartermaster with barrels of a concentrated pesticide called Superla. We issued this in quantity to the field stations where very crude but effective latrines were situated. The building was of wood siding with tarpaper or other such on the outside, a door facing away from the wind, a bare light bulb, and a row of stools from which waste dropped into a pit under the concrete floor. There being no running water, the routine after use was to drop the waste into the pit, bail a gallon of water from a barrel into the stool again and pour a cup of Superla concentrate to float on top—ready for the next client.

As was universal in the military, the latrine was a good place to "rest and visit." Often all the facilities would be in use with a waiting line, no one in a rush, enjoying the small talk and a smoke.

Well, one day we were rudely awakened from our day dreaming when an officer from the barrage balloon group came charging into the warehouse at full tilt and in good vocal projection. It took a little while before our supply officer could calm him down enough to understand what he wanted. It seems he was terribly upset that one of his men while "resting" had raised one leg to toss his cigarette under him into the stool pool. Both the warm weather and confined space had caused the Superla to create quite a combustible fuel chamber with piston effect. His man was rapidly and forcefully propelled into orbit. Some singeing and chapping was involved, of course.

The fact that others in the vicinity were not hurt and that perhaps all of them may have resolved to quit smoking and thus improve their health was pointed out to him, but he was still in an agitated state, gestures and all.

For the first few minutes of this dialog, everyone managed to keep a very serious demeanor. The more the reality set in and our minds wandered off into other "what if" circumstances concerning the use of Superla, we finally couldn't hold it back any longer. First snickers broke out and then outright hysterical laughter. No one really had been hurt, of course, and that was good. Now we were all wishing we had been present to record this historic event on film. There were dozens of suggestions for the letter we now had to compose for quartermaster headquarters. Everyone wanted to be a comic.

By the time the barrage balloon officer had time to contemplate the humor there, he, too, got into the spirit of the occasion and came up with a few doozey suggestions for the report. Frankly, it took the edge off an otherwise very dull week for all of us.

We never did learn how many of his troops gave up smoking, at least while they were "resting." Do you suppose our space program folks would be interested in a suggestion for a new rocket propellant?

The Telephone Insurance Salesman

The other day I had an occasion to receive a visit from a young, local insurance agent who wanted to discuss a new policy he had to offer. The conversation went like this...

"So, young fellow, you really think I may need some additional health and accident protection?"

"Yes, Mr. Hodson I really do. After all, what if you should become sick or injured or disabled, this coverage would be mighty important to you, wouldn't it?"

"I suppose you're right, but why would I want to become sick or injure myself?"

"Oh, of course, Mr. Hodson you surely wouldn't want to do anything like that intentionally, after all, if you did, the coverage would be canceled anyway."

"Ah, I see, young fellow. Then what you are telling me is that this protection is for something that could happen that is out of my control, like an act of God or something?"

"Yep, that's right, Mr. Hodson, an act of God is a good description."

"Well then, if this is all up to God anyway, why don't I just make him a contribution instead of your insurance company and not get sick at all? After all, his contribution would be tax deductible, wouldn't it?"

"Well, that may be true, but I can give you a written receipt, isn't that worth something?"

"You mean, if I should cut myself, I could use that receipt like a band-aid? Oh, I'm afraid, young fellow, that wouldn't be quite as good as not having the accident in the first place, now would it?"

"Heck, Mr. Hodson, I can see you are just a stubborn old cuss and I'm wasting my time. It was nice talking to you anyway. See you in church Sunday?"

"One Shot is All you Get, Lady"

In deference to the nice folks involved, I will record this little story for posterity, leaving out the names. It really does need to be recorded.

One very dark evening a wife of one of our local volunteer firemen was making her way up town in the family sedan. The streets were unpaved in those days. One rut led towards Main Street, and another rut headed the other way. It had been raining a lot, the mud was deep and the ruts were slick. She was giving the old Dodge the gun to make it up the hill.

Out of the dark came Goosh, one of the village drunks, stumbling towards her vehicle. Before she could react, he hit the car, bounced off the side door and ricocheted into the ditch, disappearing back into the dark.

The horrified housewife drove on up the hill to the fire hall to get her husband and hysterically explained what had happened. Jumping into the driver's seat, the husband and wife spun the car around and rushed back the block and a half to see what could be done for poor Goosh.

Goosh, considerably more sober by now, seeing them coming, recognized the car immediately and jumped out of the ditch, cleared the pasture fence and disappeared into the night. He wasn't about to stretch his luck—one shot is all you get, lady!

A Hunting We Will Go

When Zeek moved to Bennett County, he had a lot to learn about local hunting and fishing traditions; but for a city fellow, we must agree, he was eager and willing to try most anything. He thought it great sport to spotlight bull frogs at night and fry a panful with eggs and toast along about daylight for an early breakfast. It took several occasions, however, before he fully understood the difference between mountain oysters and those he was accustomed to back east.

Zeek did have a problem remembering in just which sequence the hunting and drinking were to be enjoyed. So it was not uncommon for him to celebrate the catch prior to the safari. Besides contributing to becoming lost on the plains, it often led to misunderstandings with tee-totaling game wardens and bullet holes in vehicles. For instance, when Max's shotgun went off as the car hit a bump and he blew the transmission out of the car. Well, whatever, back to the story at hand.

One afternoon Zeek and his buddy were preparing for the chase, at the local bar. At the appropriate state of training, they piled into Zeek's vehicle and headed for the hunting grounds southwest of town, along the Little White River. This was a notoriously popular "road-hunting" area where they were confident they could bag an evening meal of pheasants.

As they proceeded along the section road past Marie Woeppel's farm, they spotted a covey of the darnedest, biggest, pheasants they had ever seen. Despite the fact they may have counted two for one in their condition, there was no disputing these suckers were big, man! There was no way these babies were going to get away, and as big as they were, how could they miss!?

As they piled out of the rig, shotguns blazing, they made so much noise they didn't hear Marie when she came screaming out of her house, waving her arms and pleading with them to stop shooting the animals. The louder she yelled, the more they shot. Then joyful and triumphant, they gathered up their success and roared back to the bar to brag about their prowess. There they were met by the Sheriff, who gave them a detailed explanation of the differences between young turkeys and ring-neck pheasants—and the costs pertaining thereto.

My Friends, Kenneth and Naomi

Today, March 16, 1993, my old grade school friends from Norris, Kenneth and Naomi Taft, were in to surprise me.

It seems they had decided that after all these years, they felt compelled to present me with a treat for what they thought were favors I had shown them over these last many years. I guess that might cover a lot of years since we are all advancing into that 'senior' category.

Ken and Naomi told me they had been working with leather during those dull winter months for many years. Their specialty was tailor-made cowboy chaps for their many friends. Today they walked in with a beautiful set of chaps, ready to be form-fitted to suit me. They guessed well as to everything except the fit around the legs and that is what they wanted to complete in my office.

To say the least, it was a real surprise. We closed the drapes and the door and proceeded to do the fitting. They had brought along the necessary thongs and silver to finish the job on site.

Nothing would do but for Ken and Naomi to sit down on the floor as they cut and fitted these final accessories. The finished job was great! My name in black leather on one leg, crossed black pipes on the other. The fact that I didn't even have a horse these days was the subject of their jokes. Ken graciously offered to provide one any time I wanted to come visit them at their Norris ranch.

After the fitting was over, the handshakes completed and my very inadequate thanks offered, they picked up their tools and left for home.

Ken and Naomi stopped off on the way home for a visit with another old-time friend. They had supper and headed for the ranch, where, upon entering their home, Ken sighed and remarked to Naomi that he had run out of gas—and passed away. I just don't have the words to properly complete this story. I hope you understand and feel with me.

School Marms and Bank Regulators

These younger folks who arrive these days to express their authority and enforce these new Federal Compliance regulations upon us country bankers, remind me of my earlier days in the small country schoolhouse.

In those days many teachers were barely of high school age. They were usually the smallest female of the farm family living nearby, who, because of her size, was less of a necessity to the family operations and yet impressed by the needs of the family, sought to contribute to the coffers. She left high school immediately upon graduation to attend one of the 'Normal' schools nearby to take a three-month course to acquire a teaching certificate.

With this reward, she was immediately gobbled up by a nearby township school district at an amazing salary of $20 to $25 per month and a lean-to living quarters attached to the back of the schoolhouse. She carried the water from a nearby pump or spring, stoked the cast iron stove and carried out the ashes. She usually caught a ride back to the farm on weekends, weather permitting, of course.

The emphasis was on the three Rs. The school was usually a one-room building with grades one through eight. The flagpole out front was where she daily gathered the students to pledge allegiance. She monitored the recess activity, cleaned the blackboards and made sure all the students riding horses or walking, left school each evening with their homework, lunch bucket and mittens and coats.

As was the custom of necessity, work at home was a priority, so quite often the boys, especially, would be kept out of school to get the work done at home, returning to their classes again when possible. This, of course, quite often meant we would have some students who were not only older, but much larger than the teacher.

Well, as you could guess, these older, larger boys quite often felt some embarrassment and discomfort and were frustrated at sitting alongside their much younger siblings in a desk much too small and perhaps even a grade or two behind them. Such pent-up frustrations would sometimes develop into recess shoving matches or even fist fights instigated by these larger boys, all of whom were considerably stronger than the teacher. Of course, the teacher became equally frustrated. She would come running out of the school house to shout at the boys to stop, which didn't usually work anyway.

Being ignored was difficult for the teacher. There was no way to run her school unless discipline could be restored and she could impress upon her students her authority. If allowed to fester, she would lose control of the whole student body. So, knowing full well that fighting students would be dealt with later at home when their younger siblings told dad, she did the next best thing. She would smack the closest younger students with her ruler for watching the fight, order all of us into the school house and declare recess over for the week!

Now, do you see the similarity with our modern day young bank compliance examiners? If they can't handle the big guys, at least they make their point by smacking the little guy and foolishly assume it will panic those big operators into compliance also. Trouble with that is there is no dad at home to administer a licking to those big suckers!

The Stalemate Hunt

Then there was the Black Hills deer hunting trip by the local guys. They traditionally set up camp in the limestone area and camped out in tents. They always looked forward to that exciting time. It was a great time for bonding with your fellow man.

Well, one morning, as usual, they all set out for their favorite still-hunt sites. Not wanting to give away inside information about their great spots, I will avoid giving their names. Suffice it to say they did have a great, successful hunt.

One of the fellows arrived at his favorite spot and settled in with his thermos of coffee and ham sandwich. He sat with his back up against a big rock and faced upwind and into the warm sun. Every deer hunter knows it just doesn't get any better than that.

Along came a nice big buck, much sooner than he anticipated. In his able fashion, he dropped that sucker nearby under a big bull pine tree. Leaning his rifle against the tree, he took out his drag rope, looped it over the horns, threw the other end over the lowest branch and proceeded to hoist the game upwards to properly dress it out. Suddenly the buck came to—it had only been stunned. In less time than it takes to write this, the hunter was up the tree hanging on to his end of the rope. The deer snorted and pawed. The hunter couldn't get to his rifle but he didn't want to let the buck get away. He straddled the branch and kept a determined grip on that rope while that deer thrashed around. It became a stalemate.

Quite some time later, his beseeching calls were heard by his buddies, who, by now, had been searching for him. They arrived to dispatch the buck, help with the dressout and haul it back to camp. If those Black Hills bucks think they can outsmart our Bennett County hunters, they have a lesson coming!

Remember fellas, if your wife buys her own rifle and insists that she is going deer hunting with you, it's neither safe nor wise to stand in her way.

Turkey Day

Back in the '40s, the Martin Commercial Club was a lively outfit. With all the youngbloods back from service with lots of ideas gathered throughout the world, we were just about ready for any good scheme to enhance the business activity of Martin. One of which we acted upon was the 'Turkey Day.'

You see, it was like this. Among the returning veterans were some most capable pilots who were finding civilian life a little less than exciting. And while searching for some new ideas to promote the Thanksgiving-Christmas holiday season, someone suggested that we purchase a bunch of live turkeys and toss them to the gathered throngs on Main Street from their aircraft. Three local Piper Cubs were hangared nearby at the local airport. Why not give it a try?

How can anyone find fault with something we have never tried before. What the heck, this just might bring a heck of a crowd. And it did.

Come official 'Turkey Day,' right on schedule as advertised in the local weekly newspapers, an excited crowd gathered at the appointed hour at the main intersection on Main Street of Martin, South Dakota.

Meanwhile the ground crew at the nearby local sod airstrip were busy preparing the bombload. Woeppel, Wells and Tony had their crafts warmed up and idling. On signal, the co-pilot/navigator crawled in beside the pilot and they were loaded beside, between and behind the seats with turkeys with their legs tied. Off they flew, at proper intervals, one flight after the other. Military precision personified! The bombing mission was underway! We had a lot of livestock in those crates, so a number of missions were called for. And allowing a little time between each flight worked out well for the chasing and gathering of the prizes.

Now, not to take anything from our local experienced bombaiders, we need to understand here that dropping live turkeys had not been part of their training so to use a stale cliche here, we were sort of 'flying blind,' if you get the meaning.

Using the old reliable trial and error methods and flying 'by the seat of the pants,' as pilots like to relate, we completed that run-mission somewhat wiser and certainly more experienced. You see, these turkeys were not any where near as anxious about this flight as the rest of us were. To say they were a bit disturbed about sums it up. They seriously wanted to void the whole operation, and did in fact vote that way without exception. They voided all over everything nearby and handy. The inside of that aircraft may have suffered some unusual fragrances in previous rough flights, but this was for turkey 'droppings.' Our clothes, the seats, everything in range was endorsed. Dropping turkeys had taken on a whole new meaning. Take due notice, if you drop turkeys, you have turkey droppings.

As any good military yet can understand, when you are confronted with an unexpected situation, you learn to adapt quickly. And with all those happy celebrants waiting on Main Street, we adjusted the plans somewhat. The next loads were draped head down out the right side windows. The outside of the craft would be a lot easier to run through a carwash then the inside. So, loading a few less animals, but all draped outside, the second mission was on its way. At the last moment, the legs were untied and 'bombs away.' The happy, hungry anticipation was heart warming, even at the 200 feet we were making the drop from.

As you have already assumed, even though the inhabitants of the inside of that craft were eliminating the voiding problem inside the craft, those darned passengers had no idea of giving up their crude habits and had some elimina-

141

tion plans of their own—unfortunately right over that sea of happy faces. This happened after thay had been released, so you understand it was far too late for us to caution them not to do this. So it happened. We can't deny that it did happen, far too much, far too often. We were real sorry about that.

You know, expressing your displeasure with the way things are going is an understandable trait for most anyone. But it's the way these suckers selected the time and place for this demonstration that was most fortunate. We can not apologize enough for their crude behavior. I want you to believe me when I say that all of us, the Pilot and all the crew, are very sorry. But those turkeys now, they didn't show one speck of remorse. Absolutely no class. At least you might expect them to express themselves long before we got over the crowd; we did give them ample opportunity. So on behalf of the turkeys we also apologize. They just should not have behaved in that fashion.

Just one more comment on this unfortunate subject and then I will move along. For you non-rural folks, I need to put this into your perspective, lest you fail to grasp the drift here, if you know what I mean. And to be honest and fair with that noble bird, I guess we should admit that were any of us dropped without a parachute from an air craft we might also express ourselves in similar manner. But what I want to impress upon you non-rural people is the enormity of this expression. I am sure that almost all of you have, at some time or another, had contact with the overhead pigeon with very poor habits. And for you tired old military personnel, I am not speaking here about 'when the eagle flies.' We are not speaking of those dinky little dribbles from that pigeon now, we are speaking of humongous deposits by the king of America's bird life. So you see, that even country folks, accustomed to dealing with the natural habits of domesticated livestock, don't take kindly to ill mannered turkeys who adopt the bad habits of pigeons in flight, either directly or slightly upwind.

The spirit of the moment, the excitement of the chase, and the urging of the wife just do not justify the choice expletives recorded among that mixed citizenry when direct hits were evident. And believe me, our assembled clergy made their objections to us loud and clear. Turkeys or no, the trip to our happy hunting grounds was at risk here. Clean up our act, clean up the birds or find another show to put on the road. It never occurred to us what the clergy was doing out there chasing turkeys at that moment, and with that threat hanging over our heads, none of us was brave enough to broach the question.

Well, whatever, back to flight two. Here we now arrive over the target area, with dozens of innocent birds. We untie the legs, hold them away from the struts and toss them into the air. Unfortunately, that ten minute flight, head down, had the same effect upon the bird as it might have on any of us. They were dizzy as heck. The lower drops were too close to hard ground for them to regain all their senses. All they did was to express themselves as fully outlined above. Then they bounced off the closest hard object and expired, usually with some exposed internal organs and a very sad facial expression. Which, again as I say, was quite understandable if it were one of us, that is.

We dropped the birds everywhere. Some recovered before impact, some didn't and landed on rooftops where they strutted about, daring anyone to be foolish enough to climb up after them. They misjudged our celebrants, that's for sure. Flying from rooftop to rooftop eventually brought them to the outskirts of town and the footrace usually went to the populace. You have to hand it to those turkeys for a nice try, however.

The third and fourth flights and drops went pretty much as before. But it soon became evident that this project was doomed to failure. If not from the messed upon observer, certainly by the Society for Prevention of Cruelty to Animals. The Commercial Club went back to the drawing board for next year.

Not wanting to give up completely on this 'rodeo roundup' concept, the committee decided that next year it would be live birds tossed from the water tower. So, sure enough, the next year we had Elmer Simkins, the local butter, eggs and chicken mogul, buy us several crates of live critters. This time we included chickens, ducks and geese, along with the traditional and favorite turkeys.

So that year we rigged a rickety platform up the water tower leg and hauled up the crated livestock with a block and tackle. And at the appointed hour of celebration we gave those suckers the same options that we all received when our older brothers taught us to swim in the old ice pond. Toss them in and sink or swim. These citizens, fowl or not, had a clear choice when we tossed them. They could flap like the devil or crash land. Pen raised or not, we had to appreciate these feathered efforts. In some instances I am sure that some of these birds were the first to take up flying again since some distant ancestor retired that practice. The event did go quite well. And we perfected our routine very well for next year's events. For instance, we learned early on not to toss them into the wind. Some of these trophies had adopted some poor habits from last year's turkeys. The happy celebrants below had a great time grabbing, rassling, chasing and impounding every one of them!

A couple of years of hauling those critters up to that water tower platform just to give the audience some meat and those fowl some thrills got a little old. So a motion was made to return to Main Street and try something else.

So, back on Main Street the next year. This time we listened to the housewives who kept asking why the birds had to be live and unplucked anyway? So this year we tried a revolutionary concept. We spent most of the evening before the big day blowing up balloons and inserting hundreds of gift certificates inside. From ice cream goodies at Cook's Drug Store to theatre tickets at the Inland Theatre to groceries, free gasoline and, yes, free processed turkeys. These we tossed from the top of the Snyder Hotel and Darbyshire's Hardware. A high wind that day nearly did in some of the older contestants. By the time they caught up with a balloon just this side of the canyons north of town, only to discover it was for a chocolate malt at the drug store, they had physical complications that over-ruled the acceptance. Probably we would still have continued this process except for one important detail. Martin, at that point in history, was noticably

144

lacking in politicians and blowing up all of those balloons by amateurs was just asking too much. We went searching for a different delivery method for this traditional dinner.

So what the heck, despite all of our best intentions of a few years before, we slipped into the stale old groove of the rest of our over-civilized communities. We just assembled on Turkey Day at the American Legion Building where we drew names and handed out the turkeys, all dressed up and ready for the oven. Some old timers predicted that such lazy, shiftless attitudes would surely lead to a time when we would be expected to deliver the birds all cooked with potatoes and gravy!

It really didn't come to that extreme however, and here we are 40 some years later, still in that rut, giving nice dressed turkeys to lucky recipients with no strings attached, but if they want them cooked they will have to work that out themselves.

Interestingly enough, a survey taken years later (not by one of those famous political pollsters, of course) showed an interesting trend here. Statistically it was clear that chicken house raids had declined markedly after Turkey Day was inaugurated! Which just goes to prove that things can be both fair and fowl at the same time!

The Rattlers, May 1981

Son Herbert and friends captured a nice tub full of large rattlers last weekend. We couldn't use all of them, but we did locate a large two foot tall glass pickle jug with a screw-top lid. It is about 12 inches across at the widest part, so we decided to keep a dozen of the liveliest in the lobby for folks to enjoy. We didn't set it up on a stand for fear someone might accidentally knock it off and turn them loose. However, when a tourist would ask about them, we'd tell them, "Yep, we turn them loose every night in the lobby, gather them up again each morning and put them back in the jug!"

That did send a few away muttering to themselves. Some words we could catch didn't sound too complimentary to say the least. Like, "these guys are nuts" or "let's get out of here, it's almost closing time."

Well, the display didn't last too long, two weeks was all that my right-arm gal, Mary, could take before she issued an ultimatum. Her desk is in the lobby outside my office and that's where we had set the display of rattlers so folks wouldn't tease her pets. But enough was enough and Mary stated in no uncertain terms, "Either they go or I go." That was no problem at all. Son Herb took the rattlers down to his deep freezer in a plastic bag and "chilled them down a bit." In their relaxed state, he took them out and stretched them nice and straight and froze them again, hard. When it's time to process them later, it's much easier that way.

Shortly thereafter, one of the fellows from the game

department stopped by to mention he missed our live display and offered us a whole clutch of new born baby rattlers. We displayed them for a while then gave most of them away to a fellow who makes novelties with them. I kept two nice friendly little fellows, which I took with me when I attended a bank conference in Minneapolis. I just stuffed them into a plastic pint jar and put them into my travel bag. Upon reaching Minneapolis, I presented them to the folks at the correspondent bank. I am sure they were delighted! I never did hear what they did with them.

Was having coffee the other day with friend, Arnie...Arnie is one of those Harley-Davidson fans. His great thrill is cutting the breeze on a two wheeler.

Arnie swears that grasshoppers in the teeth may be exhilarating to be sure, but absolutely nothing quite compares to the big experience...getting smacked in the face with a ripe pamper when meeting a car at fifty-five miles an hour!

A Bully Story

George Cottier, old time cowboy, brings me this story, January 1984.

George tells me that during the recent all-time-record breaking cold December weather, he was riding pasture for the people now managing the old Cross-5 ranch near him.

He said he came across two of their bulls who, because of the 40 degrees below zero temperature and probably some diarrhea distress, had developed globs of frozen manure and mud nearly as big as bushel baskets, hanging on their tails. This banged against their hocks until they could barely walk and were so badly harmed they had to be destroyed.

George said he had never seen such large balls on a bull in his whole life! Knowing George, who is a very trustworthy person, I am confident this bull story is true.

One Down, One That Went

One late-season deer hunt in the Black Hills, Gene and I decided we would try for some venison. Gene wanted to try out the rifle he brought back from the Pacific and I borrowed a rifle of my brother's.

The first day we just sort of checked out the territory, didn't try hard and enjoyed the baloney sandwiches and coffee. We thought we found a likely site for the next morning up near the McVey burn area.

So bright and early the next morning we headed out there and settled in. Gene liked that lower meadow area east of the old railroad tracks while I chose a nice warm side hill facing the sun, with a big rock to protect my back, west of the tracks.

Actually, I think I had sort of dropped off to sleep when I heard a shot in Gene's direction. "One shot, one deer," we used to say, "Two shots, one deer, maybe; three shots, forget it." Since this was a single shot I assumed Gene's jungle training had paid off. I picked up and headed down in his direction.

Sure enough, about a quarter mile away, there stood Gene, covered with snow, as was his rifle. He was looking down the draw away from the road. When I asked him what happened, he explained he had dropped this deer, looped his drag rope over the horns and was pulling it into a more assessible spot to dress it out, when the deer came to and took off in the opposite direction, dragging his rope. Gene was just in the process of picking himself up from this sudden back flip in the snowbank when I arrived.

Well, sure enough, as we followed the tracks and rope-dragged trail, we hadn't gone a half mile when we came upon his buck, lying dead in the brush. I have often wondered what another hunter might have thought were he to draw down on a galloping buck dragging a rope? Do you suppose he would have thought it was a run-away from a branding?

Bless the Lawyers ,
They Provide Us with Such Good Humor

Since the good Lord saw fit to make me a short person, it soon became very apparent that my longevity dictated I perfect my running and ducking skills. It was, after all, the only wise and prudent course. Then upon reaching maturity, when the run and duck were no longer a viable defense, I decided to develop a sense of humor as a survival alternative. I do find, however, there are times, when blessed with the presence of bureaucrats and lawyers, it can become a little sticky or tense. You see, most of the best jokes these days are about bureaucrats and lawyers, and, unilaterally, these fine folks just fail to grasp the real humor of it all. Of course, it would be futile to revert back to the duck and run—that's their specialty! It's sure sad they can't enjoy the humor that they so easily provide for us!

The "Reservation Rocket"

The fall of 1991. Today one of our long-time rancher friends from the reservation was in the bank. He mentioned he needed another "reservation rocket." I had to ask him to explain what the dickens was a "reservation rocket." His detailed explanation, with tongue in cheek, was so good I hastily made some notes. Here is his explanation.

(You sure can't say our reservation friends don't have a great sense of humor!)

You will note as you travel about the "rez" that the residents seem to accumulate an unusual number of junk cars at virtually every habitable place. Usually these are parked in random, scattered in an irregular pattern, not related to any scheme of things and certainly not with an aesthetic landscaping in mind.

These junk cars are what is known as the "parts inventory" for their "reservation rocket," which is their current drivable car. They cannibalize these clunkers very well. It may surprise you to know that there are a lot of parts from GM vehicles that they can make work on Ford or Chrysler. They do have a bit of a problem with Japanese makes, however.

The current operating vehicle, if it meets the following minimum standards, may qualify for designation as a "reservation rocket." It must have:

1. At least four wheels, not necessarily of same color or size. Three tires may be bald. No spare required, no jack required. Driver's seat only required.

2. No more than one door missing.

3. At least ten square inches of visible windshield area.

4. Must run on at least 50 percent of cylinders, acceleration is not a factor.

5. Hood, side panels and fenders need not be color-coordinated.

6. At least 50 percent of fenders in place, but may be ruptured or disfigured from intended function.

7. No tail lights necessary but at least one headlight.

8. Battery optional if a good hill is nearby to park on.

9. Windshield wiper, radio and heater optional.

10. A four foot garden hose in trunk to siphon gas, which is commonly referred to as the "credit card."

11. Jumper cables preferable, but if pair not available, at least one cable needed. It is assumed that the jumper car will have second one.

12. Neither drivers license nor title nor insurance required since the rocket is designed to operate only on the "rez" anyway.

My tribal friend used to exemplify this, explaining how really active he had been all week by saying, "Hell, I've been busier than a pair of jumper cables at a Powwow!"

So long Bob We will miss you

August 1, 1985. Bob's wife was in today to settle up their account. The crop was harvested and sold. The machinery stored in the shed for the winter.

Normally this would not have been an out of the ordinary daily event, but Bob was a dear old friend of mine. We graduated together from good old BCHS, played football together, drank a little beer together and went off to military service at the same time.

Bob had the usual tough time making farming pay, just like most of our dry-land, west-river farmers. There were some good years, some very good years, but there were also the hoppers, drought, hail, winter kill and bad prices. All in all, his was a pretty typical small farmer's lot in life, but Bob always kept his jovial, happy face and manner. Never lost his optimism. Next year was always going to be better!

What was particularly unusual about Bob, aside from any other struggling farmer? Bob always had an obsession about paying his bills when due. It was very common and acceptable for us country bankers to waive an annual loan payment and look forward hopefully towards a better crop next year. Bankers and farmers know how that becomes a part of things out here.

Bob, though, insisted if the loan matured that fall after harvest, then it needed to be dealt with then. Sometimes he hustled around and sold some machinery, marketed some of his cattle-oilers invention with friend, Ed. Sometimes he sold what was left of last year's stored crop, sold some livestock, whatever. Bob made it an irrevocable practice to settle up in full every fall. He usually laughed and warned me he may be back again next week for help, but on the day the loan payment was due, it was "time to settle up."

Each time Bob thanked us for the confidence we placed in him and his operation, and always the thanks was accompanied with a firm handshake. Never once did Bob and I fail to seal that transaction without the handshake. We both looked forward to it. It made us both feel good. Well, as I say, today Jayne was in. Bob is gone now, but she paid off the family operating loan as usual. I couldn't let her go until we shook hands firmly, one last time for Bob. Then we both had to sit there a few minutes until the lumps went down in our throats.

" Damn it, Bob, old friend, I sure miss you."

The Crazy Horse Project

Summer of 1967. Another pleasant visit today with our friend, Fr. Joseph Karol, who has been working diligently over the years among the Native Americans through his position with the Holy Rosary Mission near Pine Ridge and the St. Francis Mission on the Rosebud Reservation.

Fr. Karol has managed to become a trusted and close friend of many of the tribal elders and leaders on those two reservations. He had a particularly close relationship with Mr. Morrison, an elderly fellow, living at this time on the Rosebud.

Fr. Karol explained that Mr. Morrison was the last known custodian of the burial site of Crazy Horse. Fr. Karol explained how this tradition was described to him. When a famous leader is first buried, it is usually by family members. The site is kept secret out of respect for the deceased and to avoid vandalism of the site. In the following years a respected friend of the family is entrusted with this information with instructions that upon some later date, that person is expected to remove the remains of the deceased and secretly re-bury them at another secret site, known only to themselves. When they become older and feel the time is right, they are to pass along this tradition, each new custodian being charged with the same re-burial and secret activities.

Well, Fr. Karol explained that he wanted to vouch for Mr. Morrison, so that they could acquire some operating funds to dig the last known burial site of Crazy Horse on land belonging to Morrison, being the last known custodian of this trust. Due to Mr. Morrison's advancing age, and at the urging of Fr. Karol that it was now time to make this information public and to build a memorial to this great leader on that site or near there, they had secured cooperation with others and were ready to proceed with this dig. Mr. Morrison was the third-in-line custodian and had agreed with Fr. Karol that there was no longer any threat to the remains and that it was now an opportune time to try for some sort of shrine to memorialize the site.

Mr. Morrison and Fr. Karol explained that this dig site was on the east slope of Porcupine Butte in Shannon County on trust land controlled by Morrison. I am confident they were both very sincere in their efforts to preserve the history of this great leader and share their efforts with the world. A site where Indians and others could come and pay their respects was their goal.

At any rate, in the fall of 1967 this group of people went about the exhumation and returned to the Blackpipe with a box of remains that they had removed right where Mr. Morrison said he had buried them many years before. They asked for and I made available one of our largest commercial-sized deposit boxes where once more, Crazy Horse was re-buried for awhile, pending their efforts to put the details together for the memorial.

Fr. Karol was working on this project with Dr. Leonard Jennewein, Michael Kelly of the University of South Dakota, Dr. James Pakowski of Notre Dame University, and others. The burial site was the NW 1/4 SE 1/4 Section 17, Township 37 North, Range 42 West, 6th P.M. Shannon County, South Dakota. Mr. Morrison also reflected on this in a certificate and permission form, hand-written June 9, 1968 (see transcript below) wherein he directed that any remains found were to be deposited in the Blackpipe State Bank until called for later.

In frustration with the lack of progress and because of Mr Morrison's declining health, Fr. Karol and Mr. Morrison returned to the Blackpipe and removed the contents of their deposit box. Fr. Karol corresponded with me about the project throughout 1971. It seems all their efforts to establish this memorial site on that piece of land went for naught. I assume their efforts to write a book on the subject also went astray since my promised copy never arrived. Mr. Morrison passed away and I have lost contact with my dear old friend, Fr. Karol.

"June 9, 1968
This is to certify that I hereby give permission for Mr. Michael Kelly of the University of South Dakota, Fr. Joseph Karol of St. Francis Mission, Dr. James Pakowski of Notre Dame University and any others in their party to do archaeological work on my property, namely the NW40 of the SE quarter of Section 17, T37, R42, Shannon County. Also to camp on this property.
Albert Robert Morrison"

"July 3, 1968
I give permission to have any bones found and the bones in the Blackpipe State Bank to be moved wherever necessary for scientific examination.
I want any bones found on the Porcupine Butte site to be put in a safety deposit box in the Blackpipe State Bank.
I take responsibility for disposing of the bones.
Robert H. Morrison
Witness James J. Pakowski
Bones released to Fr. Karol, 7-12-68"

Fixing the Water Line

Last evening about 4 p.m. the contractor working on the city water system shut down our water in this part of town. About 15 hours had gone by and I was getting a little tense, if you know what I mean. I hadn't slept well at all! I couldn't locate our old thunder mug. The environmentalists had long ago shut down the outhouse facility. I was seriously contemplating the foliage cover of our trees and bushes when I noticed that my neighbors were also out doing the same thing. They were furtively checking the clear view angles between themselves and the rest of us and walking sort of stiff-legged, jaw set and watery-eyed.

Well, not wanting any more trouble with regulators and bureaucrats, I decided to go down to the end of the street to "powwow" with the workmen. My Indian friends refer to such social conferences as attempts at reconciliation.

Upon arriving at the construction site, I observed a couple of young fellows in the ditch, struggling with the pipe. I explained to them that I hoped they would understand if my voice was a little shrill, that overloaded bladders often affected me in such a fashion, along with a lack of concentration and a severe headache. I further explained that despite my old age, I still prided myself on my fairly regular bowel movement schedule. At my last exam even my doctor was envious, by golly, so I wanted to continue this remarkable accomplishment. I pointed out that both of these functions had been necessarily and sadly neglected for much too long a time now. These fellows were, I must admit, very understanding and both agreed that even to a young ditch-digger, constipation was not an enviable contemplation. They were very appreciative, I thought.

Now, having their undivided attention, I gauged the distance and casually stepped astraddle of their ditch. Looking benignly down upon them, I reminisced with these young fellows about the good old infantry days when we regularly used slit trenches. It was all coming back to me now and I was most comfortable with the possibility that I could still handle such activity again should such a necessity ever arise.

Then, before bidding them a fond farewell, I explained that if I were to return shortly for another visit, I fully intended to utilize their fine ditch facility and that perhaps if they were somewhere below that activity they just might want to re-check, now, that their helmets were handy.

Well, those fine young fellows enthusiastically reassured me of an early return of our water service, and, by golly, sure enough, shortly thereafter it was back on. I guess you might say the whole neighborhood was mighty relieved. Really I was bluffing, there is no way that I could have walked that block one more time without ducking into the neighbor's lilac bushes. Old age does have its limitations!

Two Bulls-Custer May 2, 1989...

Today we had a different and most pleasant surprise. An old friend, Mrs. Eddie Two Bulls, wife of artist Eddie Two Bulls, was in again to show us a batch of Eddie's latest fine paintings about this great territory.

She was smiling from ear to ear as she showed me her beautiful little granddaughter she had in hand. She said Eddie sure wanted us to meet this little girl, so here she was!

From the big smile I knew they had more to tell me. It seems the woman and man with Mrs. Two Bulls were her daughter and son-in-law, and this beautiful little girl was their child.

She went on to explain that her daughter had been in the Marine Corps, as had this young fellow, Steve Custer. They had met while on duty together in Spain and were married.

They all wanted me to know that this granddaughter was the great, great, great-granddaughter of General George Custer!

We had a wonderful visit with this young couple and made sure they signed our guest register. Mrs. Two Bulls said that once in awhile one of the neighbors would kid Steve a bit, but she said she just told them, "Now you be nice, or I will send you home." As of this date, they are all living out on Red Shirt Table where Eddie does most of his painting.

Our Blackpipe gallery in the Blackpipe Bank lobby has quite a number of Eddie's great works which we have enjoyed sharing with many visitors. Eddie does a tremendous job of portraying the out-back country just as it really still is. He has a real talent of presenting the details that many artists overlook. I predict his works will become great collector's pieces in the years to come.

I wouldn't be surprised, however, if Eddie starts including some sketches of that granddaughter rather than just scenery pictures!

Dear Brother Herb

Just a short note today to share the events of last evening. I am sure we all have memories of events, those thoughtless things we have done, only to regret them later when we fully reconsidered.

Remember the time you forgot and tried to lick the black ice off the pump handle? How many times have we both picked up the shaving cream instead of the toothpaste?

Well, last evening, I experienced another first. It has topped all those other silly things for me, to say the least. It was exciting and impressive. Oh, yes, it was impressive and "expletive!" One of those eye-bulging, teeth clenching, white knuckling episodes. You see, half awake and in the dark I grabbed for the Preparation H and managed to locate the Ben-Gay tube instead!

For once in my life I had to agree that a string of choice expletives brought no relief whatsoever! Nor did it detract from the pain when I stubbed my toe on the door as I danced about. Even banging my head on the wall didn't help. I think that hereafter I will leave the Ben-Gay in the shed. A chilly walk, barefoot, that far might sort out my thought processes first.

Your brother, Bruce.

P.S. Believe me, this one is a real attention getter. You should try it sometime, since I know you wouldn't want to just take my word for it. You know, I haven't danced like that since Mom made me take tap dancing lessons with sister, Barbara, 60 years ago! And you thought I had forgotten all that!

The Drunk Man's Race

August 1977. As usual again this summer we had our small street fair. You know all those things that tickle the fancy of us country hicks and bore those city slickers to death? There were sidewalk displays and booths. The ladies' clubs prepared dozens of hand-churned tubs of homemade ice cream served with homemade pie. There was the baseball throw and stock tank filled with water and the local dignitaries, with whom almost everyone would love to get even, volunteering to set on that drop plank.

Games of musical chairs were played with homemade cakes to the winners. The popular cow chip toss (buffalo chips sail better) was held. There were the usual tugs of war, foot races, balloon tosses (water filled, of course). These were the tried-and-true recipes for simple folks getting together to have a good time. Of course, visits to the theatre for the kiddies to see a Disney special allowed Mom to do a little Main Street shopping while Dad hoisted a few with the boys.

Several years ago someone decided we needed a little spicing up of these activities and suggested we include a drunk man's race. The idea seemed quite popular with most of the men but not with the ladies. But what the heck, most of those same fellows would probably be in similar condition at going home time anyway. Just maybe all that running would sober them up. You can't say our gals out here aren't game for most anything interesting and different, especially when you live 40 miles in the country and have a tendency to suffer a little cabin fever. So, the drunk man's race was included in this four star celebration.

The rules for this race were simple. They had to be. Did you ever try to explain something to your favorite drunk? The police had one of those "blow in me" gadgets that immediately registers your alcoholic condition. When you line up for the race you blow in their gadget. That qualifies you or it doesn't. Last minute hasty nips were expected and allowed. You didn't pay an entrance fee, but you had to provide your own "conditioning fuel." It was really quite a fine-tuning process. Each contestant, of course, had their own limitations and maximum operating point. Now you can see why formal rules were just not adaptable here.

The distance to be run by the contestants in the race was one block. They were to run from the courthouse corner to the drug store corner where there was a rope stretched across the street. The rope was crucial. It not only gave the judges a pretty fair idea as to who won the race, but it also assured the wives that their husbands would be corralled before they got lost in the crowd. Simple but ingenious, I thought. The wives were especially impressed with this plan. In past years some of those tipsy but happy contestants went astray. A wife trying to handle two kids and struggle through that maddening throng of two or three hundred cheering spectators looking for the father of these brats could be tougher than rounding up a flock of turkeys the day before Thanksgiving in a roaring blizzard.

The race itself wasn't the big show here, you understand. You see, the particular training and conditioning required for the contestants in itself created an unusual amount of confusion in the minds of the contestants. In their inebriated condition, it was reasonable for everyone of them to believe in their hearts they were the winner! That's when the judges needed that policeman (that guy with his drunk-ometer) to bring some order here. The cheering crowd, of course, thought it great fun to encourage each contestant, those still standing, that is, and assured each one of them they had won! It was no doubt the highlight of the evening, which is why they liked to save it until the last.

Most of these arguments with the judges wound up in

good-natured resolution, usually compromised by a loyal supporter who had whipped out the stub of a jug, thrust it into the weary contestant's hand, and as far as he knew, that was the first prize! He was happy to be the winner and promised all of his supporters he would return again next year to defend his title! Of course, the judges had already awarded the $10 cash prize to the winner and he and his pals were headed for the saloon to celebrate.

This summer, our town fair went a little different. There was an official complaint from a contestant and his followers. The crowd, taking an interest in the presentation, was about evenly divided as to how best to resolve this dilemma. You see, Jumpshot was very upset when he didn't receive that $10.

Jumpshot was one of the local characters who reside in every town. They have a great life. Work when they have to, let tomorrow worry about itself. Today, if one of the gang has a place to bunk down and another one has a ring of bologna and all together they can scrape up enough for a six-pack or a jug of red wine (Ripple, preferred), then how can life be any better than that? Share and share alike, share your wine, bologna and fleas with your pals. He would do the same for me. Makes you envy them, doesn't it? Come on now, admit it!

Well, whatever, all week long we locals had watched our gang of free-spirited characters on the side streets practicing. They had run-offs-preliminaries, if you will. They always ran one block, paired off against one another, barefoot and shirtless to improve their performance. They kept at this, narrowing down the field until they all agreed that Jumpshot, shirtless and barefoot, was their best choice for the big race.

Now then, the race rules: Contestants had to provide their own state of qualified inebriation.

That was the tough part. As I explained earlier, we aren't talking about the country club set here, you understand. These free-spirited fellows didn't have an unlimited source of revenue. They knew from experience that to reach a state of legal qualification for the race,

Jumpshot was going to need a full bottle of red wine. So scramble they did. Whatever sources they could attack, they pitched in with great gusto and sure enough, they managed to dig up the $1.25 for the jug. Now they were primed and ready! They might be casual about life, but they were smart enough to know that when Jumpshot won that $10 cash prize, they had one hell of a return on their $1.25 investment. Ten dollars would go a long way in replenishing their liquid and bologna pantry. Devious suckers, weren't they? I know you can see that, can't you? Wall Street tycoons they were not, but no one should scoff at an 800 percent return, right?

On the morning of the race, the gang dug up the wine jug they had hidden in those lilac bushes out behind Cozad's Cozy Cabins and Jumpshot began to prepare himself. "Sip it easy, Jumpshot, now don't jump around too much and wear any of this off." They fine-tuned his conditioning right up to race time, man! Jumpshot was primed and ready. "Keep an eye on those judges, fellows; make sure they don't get away with our prize money!"

Then, all together, the merry gang escorted Jumpshot to the starting line. There was absolutely no doubt about his credentials. Jumpshot passed with flying colors. The Sheriff knew he would without even checking, for that matter, since he had run this test on Jumpshot and all his buddies lots of times. He wished them well, and I am sure he really meant that. You see, despite his duty requirements, the Sheriff really did envy and like his happy and harmless, steady customers who slept it off on a regular basis within his facility.

A warning shout into the nearby saloon emptied out another dozen properly conditioned contestants. As they were rounding up the qualified racers and trying to point them all in the right direction at the same time, Jumpshot's gang made a point of protest to the judges that a goodly number of the contestants were not truly qualified! Some had only sloshed some booze around in their mouths just before the drunk-ometer test, they said. But the judges had gone all through that before and they had learned from experience that you cannot please everyone. If they were to

166

take the time to pour a little more fuel into one racer and allow for its effect, then some of the other guys ready to go would be sobering up and losing ground. No, any delays were just out of the question.

At any rate, Jumpshot went on record with his objection that there were a lot of non-qualifiers around and he sure could tell a drunk when he saw one, especially those identical twins standing over there!

When the Sheriff thought he had a majority of the county's finest all headed in the right direction, he fired off a round with his police special 38 and they were off! Both sides of the street were lined with cheering supporters, anxious wives, wide-eyed kids and two lost east-river tourists.

Perhaps now would be a good time to explain the terrain of this event a little more. Aside from the usual small town emporiums and shops along both sides of the street, on the south side of the street, approximately two-thirds of the way down towards the finish line, the saloon was located. It's crucial that you keep this in mind in order to understand Jumpshot's legal argument here.

As this thundering herd of prime athletes charged westward down Main Street toward that rope, Jumpshot was leading the pack! There was no one who would dispute that fact. It was Jumpshot by two lengths for sure!

Then this terrible thing happened! You see, Jumpshot, as with a lot of those contestants, had run to that saloon hundreds of times. Why not? It was a most regular occurrence, but to run past any saloon wasn't a natural reaction for anyone of them. And sure enough, right there in front of everyone, Jumpshot just let his natural instincts take over. As he approached the saloon, he swerved sharply to his left and headed straight for the front door of that establishment, scattering spectators right and left. I know, because I was one of those innocent, but stupid spectators who should have known better than to stand right there. With all of that raw energy tearing down the street, it's a wonder someone hadn't jumped the track a long time ago.

Well, the sad part is that those other guys charged on

past and piled up in a tangle, bounded by a taut lariat rope and screaming wives. The judges, with years of experience at this sort of thing, hurriedly grabbed one out of the bottom of the pile and shoved the prize money into his pocket and headed for a safer clime, but not before Jumpshot arrived with his formal complaint. The crowd pretty much stood up for Jumpshot and the judges had to admit he did have a point there. It was simple enough. Jumpshot was running with liquor and running to win more. Wasn't it natural that his bodily functions would entertain the thought that the race should end at the Saloon? We are all drunks, right? Why would any drunk in his prime be expected to run right past a saloon!? Since Jumpshot was clearly ahead at that point, he should be declared the winner. His appeal failed. The judges melted away into the crowd. Jumpshot was crestfallen. His support team was in a real uproar. After all, they were still sober and it sure looked like they might have to remain that way for some time. At least Jumpshot couldn't complain about that.

Jumpshot's supporters left in disgust. Jumpshot stood there mumbling something about comradeship, loyalty, training schedule and things like that, but he was just standing there all alone, a sad and dejected soul to say the least.

A couple of days later I met Jumpshot sitting all alone under Cozad's lilac bush. Sober, sad and showing some nicks and bruises, it seems his buddies had demonstrated their opinion about the subject with some physical overtures. Jumpshot suggested that next year he wasn't going to volunteer again. Someone else would have to qualify; it was too risky for him!

The Canyon Wall Carving

This is an interesting photograph given me by my good friend Henry Cottier, October 13, 1965.

I have no idea as to the details of this mysterious and historic site, but it's obvious that it must have some interesting significance. It is located on land belonging to Ms. Lorraine Thomas, not far from the South Dakota-Nebraska line. It is a little southeast of Whiteclay,

Nebraska, and it requires a half mile walk from road end.

Visitors should, of course, secure permission from Ms. Thomas before entering the site. Mr. Cottier thought it may indicate the early day presence of some Spanish explorers, but that could leave a lot of room for speculation. Henry thought it may well be a grave site of one of those Spanish people.

Ms. Thomas told the following story to my son, Herbert, and Dr. Larry Gunner when she showed them the site in 1996. Many years ago a small band of Indians, accompanied by a Jesuit priest, were forced into this canyon by a larger band of hostile Indians and during the night the canyon wall was carved out by the priest. Come daylight, the small band was wiped out by the larger group of warriors.

No one with whom we have spoken knows if there has been a dig at the site to uncover any further evidence concerning the events that took place there.

1981...
We Adopt an Informal Loan Policy

After years of trying to explain to visiting bank examiners that small country banks have little need for a "loan policy" in writing, we finally caved in and adopted this informal policy on loans.

I suppose it is understandable that when examiners come out of larger cities and deal almost entirely with much larger institutions, it is difficult for them to comprehend there are still small towns where virtually everyone knows everyone else on a first name basis, and we only purchase the weekly paper to find out who got caught at what. We already knew what was going on. At any rate, it just seemed easier to get them off our case by setting down, in writing, this loan policy and dropping it into their visiting file.

I had asked repeatedly for some ideas of what they wanted to see in this formal document, but they assured me it had to be spontaneous from our own hearts. They were forbidden to dictate what exactly should be included. They would, however, study the contents carefully and judge it according to their own standards. When I was assured I had total freedom to express this policy as we personally thought best for this community, I thereupon, with tongue in cheek, called their bluff.

The following is the result. I might add that a few examiners in after years smiled, just a tiny bit, and put it back in the file. There were others, of course, including very high government lackeys, who drew a bead on us and retaliated. But that's for another book, perhaps, someday.

"Blackpipe State Bank, Martin, South Dakota
Current Loan Policy
Jan. 1, 1981

In view of the recently instituted regulations by the government OFFICE OF EQUAL CREDIT OPPORTUNITY (EOC), as applied towards banks, it may now be appropriate to adopt some sort of informal loan policy and guidelines for the BLACKPIPE STATE BANK loan officers...Therefore, keeping in mind the restrictions of the new regulations and utilizing my forty-plus years of lending experience, I have come up with this generalization memo, which we shall call 'POLICY ON LOANS'...

FIRST we should probably try to define what is a 'good' loan:

A..A loan that can accommodate the NEED of the borrower and be RECOVERED at maturity, is probably a GOOD loan...

B..A loan that provides the borrower with financial IMPROVEMENT and a PROFIT for the bank, is of course a BETTER loan..

C..A loan made just to satisfy a regulation, with obvious loss probability is a POOR loan..Even if it does thrill the borrower and bring a smile to the ECO inspector..

D..Obviously no bank can remain solvent very long however if only the happiness of non-stockholders and non-depositors is considered.

E..A GOOD loan should be collectible, in some legal jurisdiction, somewhere..

NOW..How to accommodate the above basics and make everyone happy:

1..Examine the loan request received..Bear in mind that some searching questions are forbidden, so you will need to play the detective game..(A short course in CIA subversive activities would come in handy here.)

2..Discuss the loan thoroughly with the borrower using the following basic GUIDELINES to determine...

A..Their income now or anticipated after loan closure? (see example loan No. 1)

B..Their operational needs now or later? (see example loan No. 3)

C..Their training and background, do they intend to stay in their field or expand into new endeavors? (see example loans No. 2, 3, 5)

D..What security is being offered? Is it theirs? (see loan example No. 2)

E..Is that security assignable or deliverable? (see loan example No. 2, 4)

F..Just how much equity will each of you have in that security? (see loan example No. 4)

G..What about the sincerity of the applicant? Do they look you right in the eye? (The glass eye may be the most dependable)..If so, does SHE turn you on?..If HE turns you on, hand him over immediately to one of the woman loan officers..(see loan example No. 2, 8)

H..Can they meet their repayment schedules? Or are you just going to hear those same old stale excuses again? (see loan example No. 6, 10)

I..Any references? File and forget them! Most likely those other creditors are just trying to dump him on you anyway..(see loan example No. 9, 10)

REMEMBER...If it sounds too good to be true, it probably isn't..

NOW...Sort through your pile of forms, make sure you select a dandy official looking assortment..It impresses the hell out of them..Be sure and let them know you hate this as badly as they do, but that some 'bureaucrat insists upon it'..Everyone dislikes bureaucrats and it may take their mind off the high interest rate..

The loan officer's job is never dull, even on a slow day some nut will show up with a new story you have never heard before! Such as...

A..THE ALL CONFIDENT APPROACH..."I promised my wife to take her to Las Vegas someday, and since we lost the crop anyway, I thought we may as well drive down there and pick up a little extra money..."

B..THE DREAMER.."We sure would like to buy that big new house, with the pool, so we can enjoy it while we are young enough to appreciate the bar and waterbed..."

C..THE CHRONIC.."My Doctor and my wife think that I should spend the winter down south, and so..."

D..THE ENTHUSIAST.."You see, I've got this truly great idea to make a pile of money, now all I need is this big loan from you..."

E..THE DEALER..."My brother-in-law has this hot oil deal going, and so I just thought..."

F..THE PROMOTER..."During the war, I stumbled into this old cave full of gold bullion...(now I want you to swear not to tell anyone,) but..."

NOW THEN, to illustrate these basics, let's take a typical average loan officer's day...

EXAMPLE APPLICANT 1..A nice quiet farm lady, hands show hard work..gingham dress..Middle age..Well scrubbed..Has a little place near town.. Wants to buy 50 ewes to raise sheep...You also need to know if she has plenty of feed, pasture, are fences in good shape? Does she have a good buck ram?..Since sheep generally are profitable you probably should grant this loan..NOW HOWEVER,..if that applicant happened to be a 40 year old bachelor with a shifty eye, and only displays a silly grin when you ask him if he has a BUCK RAM..Shut him off..Or send him over to a female loan officer, he's just going to screw away your profits anyway, and someone may as well get some good out of it..(Ref. guidelines A, G)

EXAMPLE APPLICANT 2..This young fellow you have known many years..Says he needs money for some mysterious 'operating expenses' to go into business with the horniest gal in town!..Don't make this loan until you determine his business relations with her..It's obvious that sound banking policy would need to know if he is her companion or business manager..(This again should be determined if possible without reference to marital status or intentions, ECO frowns on that)..Make a searching analytical inquiry..If HOWEVER he brings along the lady in question to join in this application, you will need to examine the case a little more thoroughly..What training? Experience..(Don't ask for references, the boss has been known to lead an

174

exciting nightlife) . . Expansion plans? Trade territory?.. Health?..Margin of expected profit?..Are premises attractive? (Do they need to be?) Does the location lend to convenient walk-in or drive-in traffic?..Life expectancy of security?..Should repayment schedule be set up monthly? Maybe daily??..Depreciation schedule?..And, of course is the security available to inspection? If all the answers are satisfactory, have the asst. loan officer fill in for you and proceed with the field inspection and closure..Perhaps you should monitor this loan regularly!..This could be the soundest loan you have made all day, if the overhead can be controlled! Happy customers make for a successful business operation, there is no reason why the loan officers shouldn't be happy too! (Refer guidelines C, D, E, F)

EXAMPLE APPLICANT #3..This fellow wants to buy a truck..It's obvious he is not a truck-driver, but he says that he has a friend with a truck, who will show him the ropes, and this pal has more fun on cattle hauling trips to Sioux City than anyone else he knows..App. #3 wants to get in on some of that too!..It's not really important to ask him if he is married or not, as it won't alter what he's got in mind anyway, so skip that part..You can't directly discourage this application, remember, but you could tell him about the trucker we once had a loan with, whose truck we had to retrieve from Soo City, when his wife showed up suddenly at the wrong end of the trip..And just after we probated his estate..If App. #3 still persists you might suggest he save on overhead costs by moving to Soo City and renting rooms to truckers instead..That's a 'tricky suggestion'. (Refer to guideline B)

EXAMPLE APPLICANT #4..Now here comes a clean cut, skinny little fellow who needs a loan for 'health and body builder equipment and training'..He is a very sad case, it's obvious he needs help to tear his toilet tissue..Even so, let's be inclined to find some help here for this 97 lb. weakling..Perhaps only counseling is called for here. Does he have FINANCIAL or SOCIAL goals in mind?..If FINANCIAL success is his ultimate goal, perhaps he would seek a position with the ECO people..He should fit right

175

in..If he is as strong mentally as he is physically he should do well..If instead he wants to improve his SOCIAL standing, suggest that he enter politics. "The weak shall inherit the Earth," you know. They already control Washington, D.C.! And Lord knows, there is plenty of socializing going on there!..If all else fails in this counseling session, send him to visit applicant #2..(Ref. guidelines E, F)

EXAMPLE APPLICANT #5..Every day brings in at least one village drunk..Treat him kindly, a few more months of these new regulations and you may need him for a buddy..If he has a good drunk going, and needs some extra fuel, you have two choices..Refuse the loan and he hates you..Make the loan, and he will wind up hating himself..If possible get his wife to sign also..Then she will hate you both, but she will probably see that you get paid, just so she can remind both of you about it for the rest of your lives..It's important to know if he can sign his name..(a thumbprint is legal however)..If he's so far gone that he can't hit the stool with a donut and is farting garlic out his ears, he won't remember if you refused his loan or not..BUT don't take the chance..Write out the loan refusal required..Put one copy in his billfold where his drinking buddies will be sure to find it and put the duplicate up his butt, because that's where he would probably use it anyway..(Ref. guidelines H, I)

EXAMPLE APPLICANT #6..There are always a few applicants who are pathetically in need of counseling..This applicant came in asking for money to buy a flock of chickens..Has 13 children and sure could use the eggs to feed them..Six months ago you had granted him a loan for the same purpose..Now he is back here to buy more chickens, why?..Because they had eaten all the chickens! Why? Damned things didn't lay eggs! Did he have any roosters? No, why should he? Roosters don't lay eggs!.. The counseling this guy needs just isn't about chickens, some one needs to explain to him where all those kids came from too!..(Ref. guideline H)

EXAMPLE APPLICANT #7..This guy comes in to say he has 500 cows, does all his own work, kids behave beautifully, wife adores him, they all call him 'SIR', and he is the boss around the house!..Throw the sucker out quick, a guy who will lie like that will lie about other things too..(Ref. guideline G)

EXAMPLE APPLICANT #8..Comes now the promotion expert..He has three college degrees, and sixteen letters of recommendation..He has figured out how to run a farm on manure gas, makes sandwiches out of chicken feathers and insulation from cornstalks..Great presentation, large portfolio, dressed to kill..Has an answer for everything..But don't make that smooth-tongued son-of-a-gun a loan..Hire him..Before the bureaucrats get him first..With a line like that he'd make one hell of a P.R. man (Ref. guideline G)

EXAMPLE APPLICANT #9..Comes now a delightful young lady, needing travel money..It's quite obvious that she is a little bit pregnant..ECO reminds us we can't ask if she is married..For gosh sakes, use some tact and common sense here..Remember the boss still has three wild sons running loose out there somewhere (They take after him)..Be thankful it's just a loan she is asking for, cross your fingers, curb the chit-chat, before anyone starts getting ideas, and get on with the loan closure..If you are lucky the boss might be good for another raise..If she repays the loan, take credit for great insight..If you lose the money, consider it as compassionate stupidity..You will have a lot of company with other small town loan officers..(Ref. guideline I)

EXAMPLE APPLICANT #10..Here comes the local constable..He hasn't paid the last two overdrafts, but says he needs a $500 personal loan..What to do?..You already have had two traffic citations this month..Spontaneous reaction is called for here..Take on a sudden coughing seizure, spit up on the desk, grab your crotch and run for the can!..That female loan officer can take over, and she doesn't drive anyway..Be alert, think fast and survive, that's the motto of a successful small town loan officer..(Ref. guidelines H, I)

B.B. Hodson,
Cashier, Janitor, and Public Relations"

Summer 1988

Our home in Martin faces north onto school street and we also have a street directly behind us. It's a narrow block with no center alley or anything like that. Some of our neighbors face one street, some face the other.

Just the other day, as I settled down to enjoy my evening paper, the doorbell rang, and a couple of rather pushy fellows insisted they were going to sell me some magazines. If not, could they handle my reordered magazines? Being somewhat upset anyway after a long day, I assured them in no uncertain terms that I was not interested—period! and I closed the door.

About five minutes later, I was interrupted again, this time it was the back door bell.

You can imagine that I was doubly upset to find the same two persistent salesmen, now at the back door. I am sure my voice indicated some unhappiness, when I told them no again, in no uncertain terms.

As they left, I heard one of them say, "What do you know, two old soreheads in the same block!"

Since there was no point in arguing with those facts, I let the opportunity for rebutal pass without comment and went back to my newspaper.

The Stock Broker, March 22, 1989

The gals patched through another one of those calls today. A man with a thick brogue said, "Mr. Hodson, I represent 'X,Y and Z brokerage house', surely you have heard of us."

"No, I haven't."

"Well, whatever, Mr. Hodson, what I would like to do is send you my card along with some information about us. When we think we may have something you might be interested in, we will call you."

"Sorry, young fellow, but we have use for all our available funds to make loans to our local people."

"No, Mr. Hodson, what I mean is to supply something for your own personal investment folder."

"No, thanks, young fellow, I'm not interested."

"Well, I just assumed you were a successful investor, Mr. Hodson, and as such would be interested in these good investments we offer. Surely you are successful, are you not?"

"No, by golly, young fellow. You see too many guys like you got to me in the past."

Click.

A few minutes later I had another call. I recognized the same voice again, "Mr. Hodson?"

"Yes."

Click!

These days I sometimes find it most difficult to differentiate between a broker and a bookie.

Those Out-of-Town Goose Hunters

Our family has a nice parcel of hunting ground adjoining the local Federal Wildlife Waterfowl Refuge property near here.

When we arrived one beautiful, chilly, foggy morning at our land to commence our hunt, we were surprised to find an out-of-town car parked there and some strangers occupying our pit.

The land was clearly posted that permission had to be secured from us to hunt there. We just did not recognize these people.

I inquired of the fellow if he was aware the place was posted. He assured me he was aware and that he had secured permission of the owners to hunt there.

"And who was that you spoke to?" I asked. The fellow had obviously stopped to read our sign, because he promptly responded, "Hodson said it was okay."

"Oh," I replied, "Hodson, you say? Well, that explains it. You see that's his land on the other side of that fence there."

So the fellow thanked me and crossed over the refuge fence a hundred yards and shot a nice plump goose.

I think the Judge summed it up quite well as he fined that sucker for hunting on a Federal Wildlife Refuge. He gave him quite a lecture. "You know," he said, "we really need to make an example of fellows like you. It gives a bad reputation to legitimate goose hunting!"

Now how can anyone argue with sound logic like that?

So, How are Things Up Your Way?—circa 1978

Having survived another session in the clutches of a very tall lawyer, responding to a multitude of questions during a dull and trying hearing, I am reminded of this never ending conflict between us short people and those who find it exhilarating to look benignly upon us from noble heights. This is usually followed with childish comments and questions.

Yet, I sure don't want the government to include us short people in any of their minority or disadvantaged categories and write some more affirmative action regs to protect us. Perhaps, in fact, I might even get a little pleasure out of the ability to verbally parry with the great ones instead.

For instance, the golden opportunity today of responding to this high altitude chatter almost made my day. Of course, I assumed that sucker, as big as he was, would not dare to brutalize me, especially in front of witnesses. So here is how I responded after the umpteenth insulting insinuating question.

"Sir, it is not unfamiliar to me that some tall people resent short folks. I am also sure you may find that atmosphere heady, exhilarating and exciting. We short people are not unaccustomed to a little neck strain as we respond to stupid and arrogant questions from on high. But, just so you get a better picture of our world down here, I beg to point out some interesting perspectives. We do have greater opportunities to smell the roses, a fall on the ice is seldom fatal, we get a keen perspective of nasal hair, we enjoy the clinical close-up view of female cleavages, and, by the way, were you aware that your fly is open?"

The Road Contract, July 1993

Last Monday on my way to work I got stopped again by some of my thirsty neighbors looking for a job. They needed something to do to earn a little spending money.

I told them I didn't have any work for them today. Then I thought I would play a little joke on them. So I told them I understood they were looking for someone to paint the center stripe on that 20 miles of new gravel road north of town. They took off lickety split.

Wednesday they stopped me to thank me for the help. It seems they contacted a government agency, got a grant, 10 men from the labor pool and a purchase order for 1,000 gallons of paint!

When I told my engineer brother in Texas about the story, he really blew up. "Hell, that's a waste of money, anyone should know it won't take that much paint!" Either Texas engineers are a little slower on the up take or, who knows, maybe they do stripe their gravel roads down there in Texas.

Attorney Cozad was really upset when I told him. He wanted to sue the bastards because they hadn't properly advertised for bids! But it did clear up the mystery of where that 100 gallons of yellow paint came from that was offered to me this morning real cheap!

Community Re-Investment Act

"November 5, 1993

Washington Weekly Report
Independent Bankers of America
One Thomas Circle, Suite 950
Washington, D.C. 20005

Dear Sirs:

We have been recently 'blessed' with an extensive visit from CRA..They went to great lengths to impress upon us that they were 'professionals' and that they conducted their 'sit-down' session in a "Most professional Manner"...!?

And maybe they are right..You know, we used to have some very busy ladies in upstairs Deadwood who prided themselves as being 'professionals'..And you know, the results are remarkably similar!

Come to think of it, I wonder whatever happened to those gals anyway..Do you suppose they might be working for CRA?

Sincerely yours,
B.B. Hodson, President"

Proposed Banking Legislation by Congress

"June 17, 1991

The Honorable Larry Pressler
United States Senate SR407-A
Washington, D.C. 20510

Dear Larry:

This weekend I was most fortunate to listen to a presentation on the TV of a discussion concerning the proposed banking legislation by congress...

The learned expositors were not only congressmen, but were, not too strangely, lawyers...Due to this combination of expertise they presented themselves very qualified to expound upon this subject...

The comment by them that since the international competing countries were to be envied for having 'only 200 or 300' banks, whereas our country was 'encumbered with over 12,000!' left me mystified...

Do you suppose that such profound logic might be extended to congressmen and lawyers?

Sincerely yours,
B.B. Hodson, President

cc: Ind. Bankers Assn.

An Open Letter to my Fellow Bankers

"Greetings:

I bring you great news!..I remind you that there is a much brighter side to banking! Banking does have its rewards, you know! We are all aware that we are not perfect and it's nice when we are reminded of that, so we don't slip into the proverbial rut! Like when we live too long in one community and we get too damn cozy with our neighbors and friends. 'Friends!?' Bankers should know better! We start to pat the neighbors' children on the head and give them candy! We make unnecessary loans to sick widows! We may even pay overdrafts for ministers! We spend far too much time with local charities! In general, we start to get careless and loose in our banking habits! Like, for instance, making loans to folks just because they need it! Horrors! How ridiculous! And it's no secret, for surely everyone knows that bankers can't be trusted with big decisions like that! Any bankruptcy lawyer can confirm that! But then, after all, we can't all have the natural instincts of a savings and loan manager!

I remind you of one horrible occasion when a banker actually had a neighbor's baby named after him! Hell, his own family wouldn't even do that!

But alas, fellow bankers, I have exciting and refreshing news! There is a sure cure for this slackness and irresponsibility! We call them bank examiners! Bless them!! They always show up just in the brink of time to save us! Fortunately for us, these professionals know exactly what is best for us and our community! We lived here for 50 years

185

and were too stupid to figure it all out! These amazing people seem to have this great talent even when they have only been on the job for a few weeks. They know exactly what is best for you and your people and they quickly share this with you. They let you know right off they are willing to straighten you out! Glory be!

Usually it only takes a few days in the back room, being jabbed repeatedly with a sharp stick, for these professionals to get results. It is amazing what a few well placed jabs will do! But then sometimes they may spice up your education with vague references to your future freedom or perhaps suggest that your family may really like living in a tent to affect a complete cure. But, sure as heck, they will eventually redirect your fuzzy thinking, replace your stupid frame of mind and give you a proper perspective to carry on as all good bankers should! Hallelujah!

So take heart, fellow bankers. There is light at the end of the tunnel. Count your blessings, there really are people out there who care about you! People who will show us the way and propel us firmly in that direction.

Just think how lucky we really are! Can you imagine how empty and unfulfilling our lives would be without them? Hallelujah! Praise be!

Keep the faith. Surely being a banker is not without hope!

B.B. Hodson, President
Blackpipe State Bank"

"Where Have All the Flowers Gone?"

That sad and melancholy song has gone unanswered long enough. I can now state with reasonable certainty that I have the answer.

The flowers have packed up the ashes of their draft cards and bras and stuffed this in with their Maoist red books, their pipe and their pot, slung their cute little backpack over their shoulders and moved inside the beltway!

The generation that protested, lit-up and dropped out of the establishment, are now the establishment themselves. Now it's time for the rest of America to become the drop-outs.

The big "I" has arrived as our government is rediscovered—insecure, inexperienced, intrepid and intimidating flower people are now the reinvented government.

In closing, however, I sure don't want to imply that all flowers are referred to above. Frankly, I respect roses very much. They mind their own business and suggest, with their thorns, that others leave them alone. As for daffodils and crocuses, I think a lot of them went east.

So How Can You Improve on This?

I suppose we short-grass Dakotans should envy those eastern cousins with all their cultural opportunities and cliff dwellings and their cute way of saying 'idear' for the word idea, or have I misunderstood them completely? Or their casual way of finding their way through mobs of strangers, day or night, and even in those underground tubes, where you can't look out the windows and check for landmarks. Then there is that uncanny ability of knowing just which fork or spoon goes with which dish! Man, that's impressive, isn't it? I never could figure that out.

But then, you know, strange as it may seem, I do not envy them at all! Perhaps pity is a better word.

Just think how many of them have had the opportunity of sleeping out on a Badland table top, or being lulled to sleep by a chorus of coyotes serenading the full moon. Or, for that matter, having a relaxed and intimate candle lit dinner at the Cuny Table Cafe during a spring blizzard. Or compare to the thrill of a drunk turkey race at 2 a.m. down the main street of Pukwana!

How about that skinny dipping in Bear Creek in August while you 'feel' for catfish under the creek banks? That's not to say that 'snatching' snapping turtles off the dikes at LaCreek at twilight isn't right up there, too!

Have they ever watched the sun go down over a prairie dog town full of browsing buffalo? Bet not. Or have they spotlighted for bull frogs at midnight along Stinking Water Creek? Surely they would miss the cry of the curlew flitting about that sandhills lake.

No, by golly, I think being a short-grass Dakotan really isn't so bad after all. And shucks, who needs to know tableware etiquette when we eat our mountain oysters with our fingers anyway?

Dad's Tree

When I was a young man, Dad urged me to invest some
of my earnings in the purchase of two lots across the street
from his property. It was a new part of town and Dad, who
loved trees, had already planted many trees on his lots. He

fenced them in and planted grass, but it was several years before he could start a new home for Mom.

The war came and brother Dick and I enlisted, he in the Marine Air Corps and I in the infantry.

A couple years later, Dad and Mom finally started working on their new home. Finding that one of his favorite trees was now in the way of the new house, he just couldn't bring himself to destroy it. He had George Millar, with his fresno and horse, excavate this small tree, slide it over to my lot and re-plant it there. It was a silver leaf poplar, white bark with big leaves, white on one side, green on the other. It was a beautiful shade tree, and it flourished.

The tree is now probably the largest tree in town, measuring nearly 11 feet around and standing about one hundred feet tall, shading almost half the lot. Others may have had concerns about my return, but Dad never thought otherwise. He watered and cared for the tree in my absence, noting to anyone interested that he was confident the tree would shade my home when I came back from the war.

Now I find just as Dad had often thought of me as he cared for that infant tree, I often think of him as I enjoy its pleasures while the seasons and years roll by. The birds return each spring and our squirrel chases excitedly about. The shade grows heavier as the new growth sprouts—and I think of Dad.

Birds nest their young, grandchildren climb and swing, fog drips from the branches upon the roof, songs are sung by birds and children—and I think of Dad.

We gather in the backyard under its branches for the family picnic in the cool, quiet shade of the tree, the leaves rustling and whispering—and I think of Dad.

The rains come, and while I listen to the quiet music of water dripping from the tree upon the roof and the small branches caressing my home, I drift off into a pleasant dreamland—and I think of Dad.

The storms of wind and hail descend upon us and yet the tree enfolds and protects us—and I think of Dad.

The fall arrives with beautiful colored leaves and the touch, smell and feel of winter to come, and I am comforted by the tree—and I think of Dad.

Even when the temperature drops, the winds howl and the snow piles upon us, the tree shelters and reassures us. As I huddle inside in the warmth of the house, I look out and admire that great tree—and I think of Dad.

Dad lives on with us in this tree. For like dad's steadfast dedication to our needs, his tree is always there to care for us. Standing by, strong and tall, I have learned to take its comfort for granted, just as we always depended upon Dad and often failed to show the appreciation he so rightly deserved. Tell me, how do you truly thank a tree?

I think again of Dad—and I am reminded of his tree.

Thank you, Dad.
A grateful Son.

L. A. Pier and 'Hod' Hodson started their banking careers in the Belvidere State Bank at Belvidere, S.D., in 1909.

Inside the Belvidere State with L.A. and Hod

'Hod' stayed with the Belvidere State for nine years, then decided to try it on his own, and hauled lumber down from the railroad to the Blackpipe Valley, about 25 miles south, to build his own bank. Just trails for those lumber wagons in those days. Had to ford the Big White River and several streams. Dad hired some local natives to help, and spent most of the fall and winter of 1919-1920 putting up our first bank building.

The Blackpipe Starts Up In Norris, S.D.

Orville A. Hodson
1882 - 1970

'Hod' chartered the bank July 19, 1919 and managed it well for fifty-one years.

Bank at Norris, S.D.

On January 5, 1920, 'Hod' and 'Em' opened the doors of the Blackpipe State Bank, for business . . . with a starting capital stock of $15,000, surplus $900, and $5,000 in deposits, full of hopes and ambition. Starting a new town in a fine new country . . . very few fences, no crowds, but with a few wonderful neighbors and room to grow!

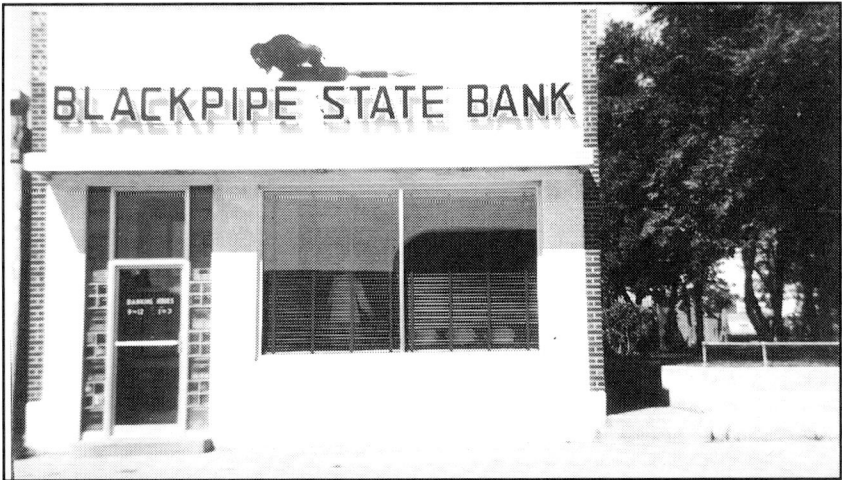

Bank building in Martin remodeled in 1947

1919   1989

In Martin, we moved to a new location at Third Avenue and Pugh Streets and built a new building in 1963...remodeling to the west side in 1972 to provide an after hour lobby and drive-up window.

Then in 1986 we built the addition to the north for additional office space and to provide a two level display gallery for our then, large collection of art, artifacts, trophies and such.

The Hodson family retired from banking in 1994 . . . some of the pictures that follow represent the Blackpipe in 1989 prior to that retirement date, showing things as they were on our 70th anniversary.

Our Trademark . . .

The local Indians used to dig black "pipe-stone" from the banks of the fine creek flowing through the valley, so the creek was named 'Blackpipe.'

When 'Hod' later saw a fine black pipe made from this stone, in the shape of a buffalo, he asked Mr. Bergen to make one for us. We have used it ever since as our copyrighted trade mark.

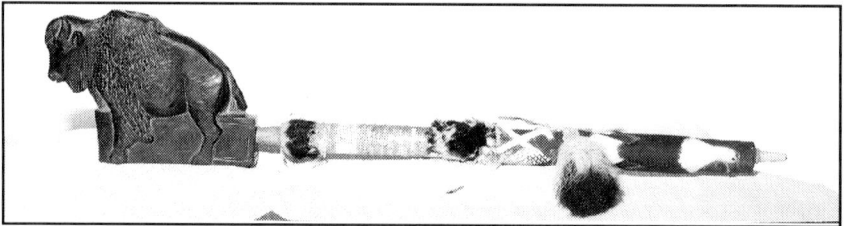

Our New Customer Lobby
1989

Some of Our Trophy Display . . .

The wildlife trophies displayed are presented by L. A. Pier, Dr. Larry Gunner, Paul Nelson, members of the Hodson family, and others.

Also on our lower level we have a display of
art work by our native artists.

Our Panorama Room Display

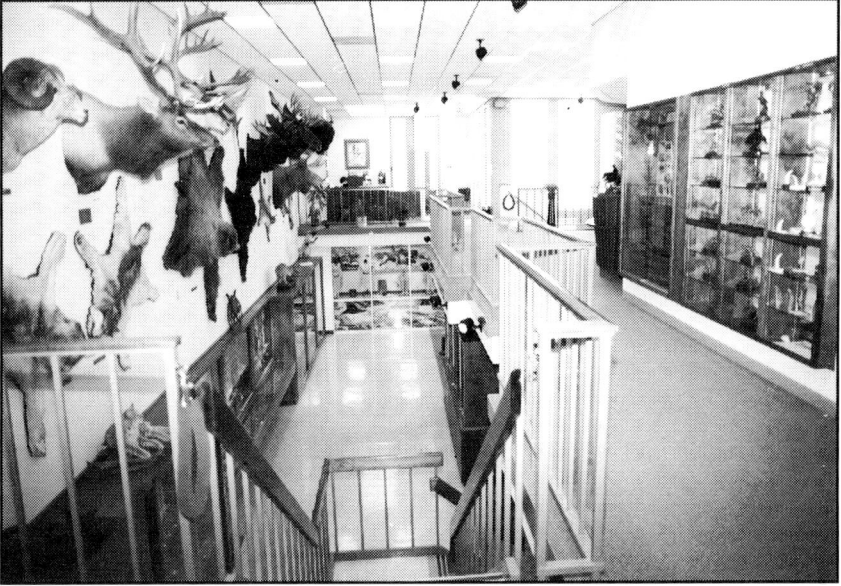

Looking into the Art Gallery

Our Staff, May 1989

Back row: JoAnn Pauly, Mary Jones, Timothy Hodson, Herbert K. Hodson, Greg Kopriva, Dorothy Hodson, and Garnet Hodson Audiss

Front row: Judy Hodson, Bruce Hodson, Susan Sigman and Nora Fuchs